I'M STRAIGHT, RIGHT?

MEN OF FORT DALE

ROMEO ALEXANDER

ROMEO ALEXANDER

Published by Books Unite People LLC, 2020.
Copyright © 2020 by Books Unite People
All rights reserved.

No part of this book may be reproduced in any form or by any electronic means, including information storage and retrieval systems, without written permission from the author, except for the use of brief quotations in a book review.

This book is a work of fiction. All resemblance to persons living or dead is purely coincidental.

Editing by: Jo Bird
Beta reading by: Melissa R

DEAN

Taking a deep breath, Dean sucked in the sharp smell of disinfectant. It was a smell he still found difficult to adjust to after months of living and fighting in the desert, but the scent of safe civilization was comforting. It beat the smell of dust and sand by a long shot, and the quiet medical wing was preferable to the sounds of distant gunfire and the occasional moan from one of the occupied beds. And it was definitely better than huddling behind a crumbling wall trying to staunch the bleeding wounds of a dying man.

It didn't hurt when the waves and wind could be heard in the distance through the open window. The ocean was only a few minutes from the clinic, and Dean was fond of walking there after his shift. The stretch of sand was far more pleasant, accompanied by the sight of water crashing against it. The ocean was the only thing that made the hauntingly familiar feel of sand under his feet bearable, and even then, he hated the gritty feel as he walked.

A shuffling sound nearby brought him out of his reverie. Turning in his chair, he looked to find another member of the medical staff poking about in one of the supply cabinets.

Troy had only been stationed at Fort Dale for three months, half as long as Dean. In the short time they'd spent working together, Dean had grown to like the man. He was a little odd but careful in his work and was good company during the long stretches the two men spent together in the clinic.

Troy looked up, catching Dean's eyes. "What's up?"

Dean cocked his head. "What are you doing?"

"Inventory."

"Inventory was done this morning."

Troy shrugged. "I'm doing it again."

Dean snorted. "Bored?"

"If I don't do something, I'll go crazy."

Dean almost wished he could say the same, but in reality, he'd learned to appreciate the peace and quiet. Sure, being assigned to a secure base wasn't the most glamorous or exciting of positions, but at least he didn't have to worry about being shot. The months he'd spent on deployment in the Middle East had taught him the value of serenity.

Dean leaned back in his seat, shaking his head. "Well, unless you've been pocketing things, you won't find any difference. We haven't had anyone come in today."

Troy sighed. "I know. Hard to believe we don't even have an exam scheduled. No fights to deal with…or anything."

Dean chuckled. "Please, I don't want another day dealing with the aftermath of fighting. Last Saturday was bad enough."

A casual observer might think Friday night would bring out the fighting since many people stationed at the fort went out for the evening. In Dean's time at the base, however, he'd discovered it was usually the morning or even the afternoon of the following day that brought the most issues. Only when everyone was hungover and grumpy did the issues start setting everyone off.

I'M STRAIGHT, RIGHT?

"I was almost convinced we'd been getting more fights," Troy said.

Dean shrugged. "Goes in spurts. Some months, you can't walk around here without tripping over someone fighting, other times, everyone seems to be behaving themselves."

Troy wasn't totally paranoid, though. Dean, too, had noticed an uptick in fights, both on and off the base. It wasn't enough for Dean to wonder what might have got into the water, but it was enough to catch his attention.

"It's no different out in the field," Dean continued.

"You'd think people would get along better in the middle of a warzone," Troy said, setting his tablet aside.

Dean chuckled. "And you'd be wrong. Sure, when you're under fire and fighting for your life, everyone gets along. When you're back at camp, though, all bets are off. Sometimes things happen out in the field that aren't settled until you're safe and sound."

"With fists."

"And a lot of cursing."

Troy shook his head. "Never going to understand that."

"You joined the wrong government organization then. Cram a bunch of guys together, and the testosterone will fly. When it does, that's where we come in. Either because someone decided to settle a problem by throwing a fist or because some genius got the bright idea to dive into a pool from a second-story balcony," Dean said with a grin.

"Didn't someone do that last week?" Troy asked.

"Yep, forgot to aim for the deep end. Dumbass is lucky he only bumped his head instead of snapping his neck. God looks out for drunks, toddlers, and privates trying to show off, I swear," Dean said with a shake of his head.

Troy glanced over Dean's shoulder. "What are you up to anyway?"

"Pretending I'm going over the appointments for the week and resupplying."

Troy sighed. "Probably a good idea. I don't need old man Winter on my ass about not having enough supplies again."

Dean frowned. "Don't call him that. General Winter is probably in better shape than you despite being twice your age."

"He's also a hard ass."

"Only to people who are a pain in his."

Troy stuck out his tongue. "Kiss ass."

Dean rolled his eyes, choosing not to dignify that accusation. While it was true he had a great deal of respect for General Winter, the man he reported to and the man in charge of Fort Dale, he didn't see it as brown-nosing. He was the youngest general Dean had met, being in his early forties, and probably the youngest he'd heard of. Anyone capable of earning a high rank at such a young age was more than worthy of respect in Dean's eyes.

Troy plopped down on the edge of the desk. "How long do you have?"

"Another hour," Dean said, glancing at the clock on the screen.

Troy groaned. "I'm pulling a double."

"I did that pretty much all last week. You'll survive, I'm sure," Dean said.

"What are you doing after you get off?"

"I've got a dinner date."

Troy's eyes widened with delight. "Oh? So I take it you and what's his name worked out pretty good then?"

Dean scoffed. "Marco and I worked out three weeks ago and have been working out ever since. Where the hell have you been?"

"Apparently not in the loop," Troy said, scooting forward.

Dean groaned, looking around, hoping to find something

I'M STRAIGHT, RIGHT?

to distract Troy. It was ultimately futile, as there wasn't anyone in the small, curtained-off cubicles for Dean to send Troy to check on. The entire building was empty except for them, and Troy didn't look like he would be dissuaded from being nosy.

"Are you guys serious yet?" Troy asked.

"After a few weeks? What is this, high school?" Dean asked dryly.

Troy snorted. "A few weeks is a perfectly reasonable amount of time to get to know someone well enough to say if you want to commit to something more serious."

"Not when you're constantly working double shifts, which, to be fair, Marco and I both do," Dean pointed out.

Troy screwed up his face in thought. "True, I guess you are pretty busy. What's he do again?"

"Tech consultant. He landed a nice position at one of the security companies further inland."

"Oh, smart, *and* makes good money. Damn, you're in business if he's good-looking too."

Dean did not want to be the one to tell Troy that Marco was, in fact, quite handsome. Troy made it his business to be involved in everyone else's business and, for some reason, took a particular interest in their love lives. The others working in the clinic were usually safe, either because they already had a steady relationship and thus weren't all that interesting to Troy or because they didn't give him as strong a reaction as Dean.

"And what's Sloane think about this?"

Dean frowned. "What's Sloane got to do with it?"

Troy raised a brow. "I mean, the guy's your best friend, isn't he?"

It was true, he and Sloane had met in boot camp, and from then on, the two of them had been close. Fate seemed to conspire to keep the two of them around one another, ensuring they were transferred to the same bases. Even when Dean had been deployed, Sloane had ended up deployed to the same desert outpost, though on an entirely different squad. They were never assigned to the same team, duty, or anything too close, but they were never too far apart. It had been a relief, though not unexpected, when Dean arrived at Fort Dale after his deployment, only to discover Sloane was already there.

"Yeah," Dean said, forcing his jaw to relax.

"Well, unless you guys have a different kind of relationship than what other people call friendship, I imagine he'd have an opinion."

Dean shrugged. "Not really."

Troy snorted. "I find it hard to believe Sloane doesn't have an opinion. The guy's got an opinion on everything, and it's usually a foul one."

"Don't be an ass," Dean told him.

"Am I wrong?"

"He's not that bad."

Dean tried not to let Troy's eye roll get the better of him. Sloane wasn't the easiest person to get along with, but his best friend had a good heart. It was just buried beneath a foul attitude and an even fouler mouth. Many people were willing to look past the surly expression usually planted on Sloane's face, with at least half of them willing to do so because of the man's looks. Having known Sloane for almost six years, Dean was pretty sure his friend had no idea how attractive he was. What Sloane did know was his looks tended to lure people closer to him, much to his irritation.

"Anyway, he doesn't know," Dean said.

"Wow, don't you guys share everything?"

Not everything, though it wasn't from a lack of wanting on Dean's part. In the early days, he would have happily shared a bed with Sloane. Even in boot camp, Sloane had been big, and his time serving had made him into a veritable slab of muscle. With pitch-black hair, flashing green eyes, a jawline that could cut glass, and a low, rough rumble for a voice, Dean could unashamedly admit Sloane was sex on two legs.

Once Dean got to know Sloane better, the sexual element of his thoughts had eased, though never disappeared completely. The more he'd seen of Sloane, ignoring the grumpiness while also knowing when to cut through it with bite of his own, the more his feelings for Sloane changed. Lust and desire had grown into an intensely close friendship and, eventually, something Dean could only call love. Everywhere they went, people commented on their bond, and Dean could easily see himself spending the rest of his life with the man.

Except, Sloane was completely, utterly, and hopelessly straight.

"I'm not going to go running to him every time I go on a date," Dean finally told Troy, turning away to face the computer.

Troy leaned back as though sensing he was treading on dangerous ground. "Look, I know what I said a minute ago, and I mean it. Sloane is a grumpy fuck who's just as willing to knock you over the head for looking at him wrong as he is to ignore you completely when you talk to him. But he's not like that with you, and heaven help anyone stupid enough to talk shit about you when he's within earshot. The dude is really protective, and he obviously gives a shit. Just seems like something you'd tell him."

Dean breathed, pushing away the familiar but faint pang of longing. How many times had he seen the same behavior from Sloane in the past and hoped it meant there was a chance for them? The nights Dean had spent analyzing everything Sloane said and did that day, hoping for a sign, looking for a clue that his dreams might come true. It had taken him years to learn how to move past that, keeping hold of his close bond with Sloane at the same time, that he could only now ignore the feelings and move on with his life.

Hence his budding relationship with Marco.

"Well, that's exactly why I haven't told him about Marco yet. I don't need him getting stressed out because I'm dating when I don't even know if it's going to be anything serious," Dean said, opening the spreadsheet again to keep busy.

"But you're going to tell him if it does, right?"

Dean glanced over his shoulder, smirking. "For someone who doesn't like Sloane very much, you seem worried about him."

Troy wrinkled his nose. "Look, if he gets pissed off, everyone around him is going to suffer, and probably the people around you too. I just don't want to get punched."

Dean smiled sweetly. "If you were worried about that, you wouldn't constantly be sticking your nose in my dating life."

Troy hummed, holding his hands out. "I promise I shall endeavor to maintain a more professional and respectful relationship with you from here on out, and I shan't enquire any further."

Dean looked unimpressed. "Uh-huh, until tomorrow, or more likely, when a new question hits your tiny brain."

Troy's eyes widened. "Speaking of…have you guys screwed yet?"

Dean picked up a nearby binder and smacked Troy across the knees. "Out! Go scrub the bathrooms, find cobwebs, walk into the ocean, I don't care, out!"

Troy darted off with a laugh before Dean could find something to hit him with in earnest. Dean glared at his retreating shadow before returning to the computer. He swore, one of these days, he was going to find a way to keep Troy quiet for at least ten minutes a shift.

His attention was pulled toward his phone, which blinked its silent alert. Opening the screen, he smiled softly at Marco's name above the text notification. The man was confirming their date in a couple of hours, and Dean tapped back his response. They were going to some Thai place Marco was a fan of and swore up and down Dean would like, right before the hot food burned him out. Dean, who adored spicy food, took that as a personal challenge and was looking forward to the little competition they would have.

Dean had no sooner set the phone down than the thump of the doors to the clinic being thrown open jerked his head up. His heart hammered, and he only managed to unclench his fist when annoyed cursing and footsteps could be heard. Troy appeared in the doorway, rolling his eyes.

"Shot himself," Troy grunted.

Dean stood up. "What?"

"With a bag round," Troy added.

"A...those bags of beans...for practice? How did...never mind," Dean said, pushing past Troy to deal with whatever soldier had just stumbled through their door.

Just another day.

SLOANE

⦻

"Look at the ass on that one."

Sloane grunted at the words but gave no further reaction. His thick fingers tapped at the phone screen as he typed out a message to his sister. Why she felt he was the one to come to when she was having boy troubles was beyond him, but he couldn't ignore her when it sounded like she was half a step away from hysterics. Sloane would have happily dealt with the problem in person in his own way, but he was pretty sure he'd end up in jail if he terrorized a fifteen-year-old boy who probably didn't know his head from his ass, let alone how to treat a woman.

"Seriously, look, before she's gone!"

Annoyed, Sloane looked up to see what all the fuss was about. His eyes fell on a woman jogging past the front gate, nearly out of sight. Sure enough, she was wearing what Sloane thought were probably yoga pants, though he wasn't sure those were the best choice for a jog.

His companion elbowed him. "See?"

Sloane leaned away, glaring at Private Simmons. "Yeah, great."

I'M STRAIGHT, RIGHT?

Private Johnathon Simmons rolled his eyes. "You're no fun."

"It's a nice ass. What else do you want? Am I supposed to be drooling over it like some middle schooler?" Sloane asked.

"A man can appreciate a nice ass at any age," John said, looking like he was trying for dignified but falling short and looking pouty instead.

"Appreciating isn't the same as drooling. Told you that when you creeped out the last girl who went through here," Sloane grunted.

"I was flirting."

"You were fucking creepy."

"You just don't get it."

The third member of their front gate watch trio, Trisha, snorted. "He gets plenty."

Sloane turned his glare on her. "Thanks."

Trisha shrugged, barely acknowledging his foul expression. "When it's true, it's true."

John sniffed indignantly. "Well, not all of us are gifted with stupidly good looks, alright?"

Sloane rolled his eyes, returning to the conversation with his sister. He would much rather deal with her drama than listen to Simmons whine about how he couldn't get lucky. It didn't matter what anyone tried to tell the private, Simmons would continue bemoaning his fate, never once considering that *he* might be the problem. If he wanted to moan, groan and carry on, that was his business, but Sloane wasn't willingly going to feed into it.

"Sloane looking good is only half the battle. The fact that he doesn't treat every woman like a starving dog treats a pork chop is the other half," Trisha shot back.

"I do not! Plus, how is it fair that just because I show an interest, that's a bad thing? He just grunts at everything, and they fling themselves at him."

"Hey, some people find the grunting sexy."

"Only because they don't have to work with his crabby ass."

Sloane looked up, glaring. "Only people who complain about me are jackasses like you. Quit your whining."

John jabbed a thumb at him. "See?"

"I mean, he's not wrong," Trisha said.

"I'm not either."

Trisha shrugged. "No, he's a grump, that's Sloane, you get used to it. You've been stationed here what, a couple of weeks? You'll learn to love his glares and insults right along with the rest of us."

Sloane eyed her. "Quit encouraging him, or he'll never shut up."

"I like hearing him whine. Gets me all tingly inside."

John flopped back in his seat with an annoyed grunt. "Is that the answer? I just have to let women torture me, and then I'll have their attention?"

Trisha winked. "Maybe you should try it."

Sloane finished the rest of his message, desperate to block out the chatter from his companions. Why General Winter thought Sloane needed to be posted at the front gate and stuck with two other people was beyond his understanding. Sloane wouldn't consider himself a paragon of introspection, but he knew himself well enough to know he wasn't a people person. People didn't like him, and most people drove him absolutely crazy.

John glanced at him. "Who're you talking to anyway?"

"Don't start sticking your nose in my business just because you can't get laid," Sloane grunted.

"Hey!"

"It's probably Dean," Trisha said, returning to the book in her lap.

"Dean?"

"The Doc."

John's eyes lit with realization. "Oh yeah! I forgot you two were friends."

Trisha picked the book up with a shake of her head. "You have the attention span of a gnat."

"Wait, but isn't he like...you know," John began, waving his hand around in a vague fashion.

Sloane looked up. "Isn't he what?"

John gestured emphatically. "You know."

Sloane knew exactly what John meant, but he wasn't going to make the conversation any easier on the private. Sloane wished he could have been paid for every time some smart-ass decided to comment on either Dean's sexuality or their friendship. He would have had a nest egg waiting for him to make a strong start in civilian life once he was done in the military.

John stopped, cocking his head. "Wait, how does that work?"

"How does what work?" Sloane asked with a growl.

John frowned. "How do you get all these girls? That ain't fair?"

Trisha sighed. "Oh, boy."

"I'm not gay," Sloane said.

"Yeah, but—"

Sloane narrowed his eyes. "I'd ask you if it would be any different for you to be friends with a woman, but I don't think you know how to be around a woman who isn't Trisha without acting like a fucking idiot."

"Only because I'll break his fingers," Trisha piped up.

"Just because I'm friends with Dean doesn't mean I'm with him," Sloane continued, ignoring her.

John wrinkled his nose. "Isn't it...weird, though?"

"How the fuck would it be weird? It's called being friends. You have those, don't you?" Sloane demanded.

"Well, yeah, but they're not, you know—"

"The word is gay. You can say the word without suddenly wanting to have a dick in your mouth," Sloane growled.

Trisha snorted, but John's frown only deepened. "You don't worry about him like, trying to hit on you, or get with you, or like...you know."

Sloane set his phone down on the desk and leaned forward, dangerously close to the private. "Just because you don't know how to exist around the gender you're attracted to without acting like a fucking pervert doesn't mean everyone else can't. What he does or doesn't do isn't any of your goddamn business, and if you don't want to end up losing a few teeth before the end of the shift, I advise you to shut the hell up about him."

John's eyes widened, and he visibly leaned away from Sloane. "I...alright, touchy subject."

"It isn't touchy until someone gets stupid enough to run their mouth. Now fuck off and go check the fence or something. I'm tired of looking at you," Sloane snarled.

John opened his mouth and glanced at Trisha, who subtly shook her head and thought twice about whatever he was going to say. With wide, wounded eyes, he pushed out of his seat and stomped out of the booth that served as the main gate to the base. Sloane watched him go, glaring at his retreating back and not letting himself relax back in his seat until John was out of sight.

"Dumbass," Sloane grunted, snatching his phone back up to read his sister's reply.

"Gotta give him credit. He looked like he was going to finish what he was saying, even with you ready to rip his lungs out," Trisha said, flipping to the next page.

"I don't have to give him credit for shit," Sloane grunted.

"And, of course, he won't keep his mouth shut."

"Fine, let him tell people. Like I give a shit."

"Which is only going to add to the rumors."

Sloane looked up, wondered if he wanted to know, and finally gave in. "What rumors?"

Trisha looked up, her thin brow raised. "That you and Dean are more than just friends."

"Oh. That," Sloane said, turning his attention back to his phone.

From the moment he and Dean had become friends, the rumors about what he and Sloane were actually up to when no one was looking had started. They bothered Dean more than anything, which Sloane thought was weird as hell. He didn't give a shit what anyone thought he was up to. He had nothing to prove to any of them.

"You would make a cute couple," Trisha added.

Sloane sighed. "Don't fucking start."

Trisha chuckled. "You would. You have that big, manly, grumpy thing going for you, and Dean is...well, the doc is Doc."

Sloane turned a scowl on her. "You saying he's not manly?"

Trisha didn't even blink. "There's manly, and then there's Sloane, six-plus feet of pure muscle, tattoos, and growly barking manly. Truth be told, it's a little weird thinking of you with a woman or at least a really feminine one."

Sloane blinked. "Excuse me?"

Trisha shrugged. "Putting someone girly with you seems weird."

"This is the weirdest conversation I've had with you, and I'm not even sure what the fuck we're talking about now."

"Really? After almost eight months of working with me, this is the weirdest?"

"It's close."

It was hard to believe he'd been assigned to Fort Dale for only eight months and even harder to believe it had been mainly spent on guard duty. How he'd gone from a soldier in the field, leader of his squad, to manning a hut on some far-flung base was a mystery.

Sloane rubbed his brow. "I don't care if people start talking about Dean and me being something, alright? It's not true, but it's not going to stop people. Just fucking wish people could mind their own business."

Sloane was comfortable with who he was and with who Dean was. What did it matter to him if Dean was attracted to guys? All that meant to Sloane was that it would be useless to talk about women with him if he even wanted to. It wasn't like Dean had been dating while they'd been friends; he was too busy working or deployed.

The two months Sloane had been taken out of the field and posted to Fort Dale, while Dean had continued to be deployed, had been lonely. Sloane had been ecstatic when he learned Dean was not only coming stateside but that he was being assigned to the same base. That was until he'd seen Dean for the first time, and something had been...wrong.

Trisha shrugged. "I don't care if you two are an item, banging quietly on the side, or simply cuddle buddies. I'm just telling you what everyone else is going to say."

"They've been saying that shit since boot camp. I don't give a fuck. Dean's a good guy and my best friend. Everyone else can fuck right the hell off," Sloane snapped.

Trisha looked up again. "Need an aspirin?"

Sloane pulled his hand away from his forehead. "I'm fine. It's just a headache, probably from the stupid conversations I've had to endure today."

Trisha hummed thoughtfully. "How's the family?"

Sloane glanced at her, unsure if he should be relieved that she was changing the subject or suspicious. He'd been working alongside her long enough to know the woman was far more devious than her casual demeanor let on. Then again, more than many people he dealt with save for Dean, she knew how far she could push him before he lost his patience.

"Fine. Shawna's learning what dating is like," Sloane said, easing back into his seat.

Trisha chuckled. "Poor thing. I remember dating at that age, don't recommend it. And how's big brother dealing with it?"

"I'm just fine. Thank you very much."

"Really?"

Sloane looked up. "I'm not some asshole who's going to go barging into her business."

"Really?"

"Shut the hell up."

Trisha chuckled. "You and I both know you're very protective of the few people you let yourself give a shit about."

"And I can't do anything from here, now can I?" Sloane asked.

"But you can text her," Trisha noted.

Sloane shrugged. "Best I can do at the moment. I will call her later, though, to ensure she's alright. She's a good kid, got a good head on her shoulders when she can remember it's there. Sucks for her now, but give it a few weeks, and she'll realize it's not a big deal."

"And probably have found another boy to do the same thing with," Trisha said.

Sloane wrinkled his nose. "I hope she learns better than that."

"When it comes to matters of the heart, nobody learns," Trisha said.

Sloane sighed, unable to argue with her logic. He'd gone through his own trials regarding romance when he was younger, and he supposed everyone had to go through it at some point. In many ways, he'd been like a parent as much as a brother to Shawna when she was growing up and, to a lesser extent, his other sister. Sometimes, it was difficult to accept he couldn't do much for them except be a shoulder to cry on and a listening ear.

"And your mom?" Trisha continued.

"The same as always. I keep trying to get her to take some time off, but she won't," Sloane grumbled.

"Mmm, stubbornness is a family trait I see."

"She doesn't need to work as much as she does anymore. Between Lena and me contributing, she shouldn't be working herself so hard," Sloane said.

It had made sense when Sloane had been too young to do much more than grab the occasional odd job. But with him and his sister old enough to have full-time jobs so they could contribute, and his youngest sister being the only one left in the house, his mother should be less hard on herself. Yet, she was not a woman to be deterred so easily. Sloane could confidently say his mother should no longer be working sixty-hour weeks as she had when he'd been younger.

"Maybe she likes being busy," Trisha offered.

"Or she just likes giving me a headache," Sloane grumbled.

"It's a mother's prerogative to torment her son, or so my mom likes to tell me," Trisha said.

Sloane eyed her. "Please tell me you're not the one working the double with me tonight. I'm not sure I can handle any more of this heart-to-heart."

Trisha looked up from her book. "Nope, going out tonight, but you and John will be best buddies all night."

Sloane stared for a moment before leaning forward to check the roster. Sure enough, Simmons' name was right there next to his, all the way through to morning.

Sloane groaned. "Damn it."

DEAN

Spinning the pen on the desktop, Dean shifted his phone between his face and shoulder. Grabbing the computer mouse, he opened the schedule for the day, looking it over.

Marco chuckled in his ear. "Gotta say, I was a little impressed that you beat me."

Dean grinned. "I told you, nothing gets between me and good food, not even a whole lot of spice."

"Not even my family can eat more curry than me," Marco said.

Dean smirked. "Well, now you have someone who can outdo you."

"Well, in one way anyway."

Dean glanced over his shoulder, making sure Troy wasn't around. "If I recall correctly, I was keeping up with you just fine in that too."

"True. For someone who hasn't been with anyone in a while, you certainly didn't seem to have too much difficulty."

That wasn't strictly true, though Dean wouldn't correct him. In the six months Dean had been back on American soil, he'd taken a few opportunities to have fun. No one said that being madly in love with your best friend meant you couldn't get laid, and in fact, Dean had found it helped. He wasn't going to tell Marco about his liaisons, however, any more than he would tell the man about his complicated emotional relationship with Sloane.

Dean leaned back in his seat, grinning. "I guess I made a good impression then."

"That's one way of putting it."

"Hey, you're not alone. I found myself a little impressed too."

"Well, that's always good to hear. A guy likes to hear when he's doing things right."

Dean wasn't going to argue. He and Marco had only been seeing one another for a few weeks, and last night had been the first time Marco had made a real move. Sure, the man hadn't wasted the chance to get in a good kiss on their first date, and a few instances of kissing and heavy petting reminded Dean of high school. Yet Marco had waited until the night before to try anything further, which Dean considered a mark in his favor.

And despite the worries and doubts in the back of his mind, he'd enjoyed himself.

Marco chuckled. "I think the real question I have to ask is, when do I get to see you again? Unless you were planning on loving and leaving me."

Dean laughed. "You're right. The past three weeks have just been me waiting to get into your pants. I'm just using you for your body."

"I'm going to take a leap of faith here and say you're full of shit."

Dean grinned. "You're right because I'm actually using you for your knowledge of excellent food places. Seriously, that's four dates now, and the food has never been anything short of amazing."

I'M STRAIGHT, RIGHT?

Marco let out a laugh. "My mom always told me the way to a man's heart is through his stomach."

"And his pants, it seems," Dean said.

"Eh, truth be told, I've found that's not the hardest part of a man to get into."

Dean snorted. "Well, something's hard."

"And what fun when it is."

Troy's voice quipped from behind Dean. "Oy, which one of your boyfriends are you chatting with now?"

"Boyfriends?" Marco asked, sounding amused.

Dean rolled his eyes, glad he'd warned Marco about some of the people in his life ahead of time. It was hard enough for Dean to put himself out there and date someone else. The last thing he needed was for someone's big mouth, say Troy's, to come along and ruin the whole thing with some stupid comment.

Dean turned to Troy. "Don't you have a job to do?"

"Yeah, but I figured I'd warn you that your other boyfriend is heading this way. Just spotted tall, dark and grumpy out the window."

"I'm guessing he means Sloane," Marco guessed.

"The one and only. He's got an appointment today," Dean explained, logging out of the computer and pushing up from the desk.

"Dare I ask when I get to meet him?" Marco asked.

Dean winced. "I would really prefer you and I deal with...you and me before I bring anyone else into the mix."

"One of these days, you're going to have to tell me the story behind you two," Marco said.

Dean blinked. "There's no...story. We're friends. He's my best friend."

"And all friends have stories. Hey, don't worry about it. I was trying to give you a hard time, okay? Text me when you have a free minute later, alright? Maybe we can compare schedules and try for date five. Might be my lucky number," Marco offered.

"Yeah, I can do that. Maybe you can introduce me to something I haven't had yet."

"That'll be a feat. I'm pretty sure you've had everything possible."

Dean chuckled, letting the man get off the phone so he could face the rest of the day. He knew Marco was aiming toward something more serious between them. Something that wasn't just casual dating. The thing was, Dean wasn't sure how he felt about that and kept putting off thinking about it too hard.

He knew there was no point in hanging onto the delusions about him and Sloane, so he'd forced himself to start dating again for the first time since he'd left for boot camp. On the other hand, some part of him wasn't willing to let go just yet. In truth, he hadn't expected to find someone like Marco when he'd put himself back on the market, and it was complicating things in Dean's already cramped head.

A familiar growl echoed down the hall. "Get the hell out of the way, Troy."

Troy sighed. "Sloane, c'mon, just...let me do this real quick."

"You can sign me in without asking me the same stupid questions you ask me every time. The ones I answer the same way every time. Just put in the same answers."

"That's not how this works."

"Sure it is, or did you forget how to write?"

Troy sighed. "Dean?"

Dean chuckled, stepping out of his cubicle and into the main hallway. Troy stood under the shadow of Sloane's hulking form. Troy was looking sufficiently annoyed while still managing to look unnerved. Dean was used to people being put off by Sloane, who was as scary acting as he was scary looking. When Dean had first spotted Sloane in his group at basic training, he'd thought the guy was the meanest son of a bitch Dean had ever seen and pitied the man who ended up partnered with him.

Only for it to be him.

Dean smirked. "Problems?"

Troy huffed. "Can you deal with this?"

Dean winked at Sloane. "Answer the nice man's questions so we can get on with this."

Sloane rolled his eyes toward the ceiling and kept them there. "I've been sleeping fine. No weird pain or thoughts. My mood is the same as it's always been, and no, I haven't wanted to kill myself. Happy?"

Troy perked up. "And have you had any dietary changes we should know about?"

"Yeah, I'm a fucking vegetarian now," Sloane said.

Troy looked down at his tablet, nodding. "Right, no changes there. Alright, then I'll leave you in Dean's capable hands and go busy myself as far from your evil glare as I can without getting my ass in trouble."

Dean glanced down the hall toward the front door of the clinic. "You mind sweeping?"

Troy's steps hesitated. "Again?"

"I've already done it six times today. You've done it once," Dean pointed out.

"You and your obsession with keeping the sand out," Troy huffed.

Sloane closed his eyes, and Dean waited until Troy had hurried out of sight before speaking.

"You know he's just doing his job."

Sloane eyed him. "If something was different, I'd tell him. Don't know why we have to do this every time I come in here."

"Because the military likes their lists, and they like their lists to be followed, or we get our asses chewed up one side and down the other."

"You could always fill it out for me. No one would know any different."

"Yes, but then how would I terrorize him and annoy you?"

Sloane grunted. "Fine, mission accomplished."

Dean chuckled, motioning to the nearest curtained cubicle. "C'mon in."

Sloane walked to where Dean had indicated and began pulling at his clothes before Dean had drawn the curtains. Dean didn't bat an eye, used to service members and their complete lack of aversion to nudity. Basic training destroyed most of the modesty a soldier might have, and deployment took care of the rest. Most men he treated or looked over were no different from Sloane, stripping down to nothing without thinking about who might be around. The clinic's privacy curtains were as far from their minds as it got.

By the time Dean had drawn the curtain around the cubicle, Sloane's shirt was off and he was shimmying out of his pants. Dean realized he'd left his tablet back at the desk but shrugged it off. Even at first glance, he could tell not much had changed about Sloane since the last exam, and Dean would have heard about anything abnormal from Sloane's lips beforehand.

"At least you wore underwear this time," Dean commented, waiting for Sloane to hop on the table.

Sloane smirked. "Wouldn't want to make Troy feel bad again."

Dean rolled his eyes. "That's my favorite thing about you, how humble you are."

"And you had me thinking it was my sunny personality."

If there was anything Dean could say about Sloane, it was that his friend possessed great self-awareness. Sloane knew he was a surly bastard, he just didn't care. Yet, he also knew he wasn't lacking in the looks department, but didn't particularly care about that either. Despite his beautifully bronzed skin, a mixture of his time spent in the sun and his Latin blood, a musculature that was both impressive yet not too much, and features that were rugged without being blocky, Sloane was never arrogant or stuck on himself. In truth, sometimes Dean wondered if Sloane was even aware how attractive he was.

Thankfully, in this setting, Dean was immune.

Dean snagged Sloane's arm, turning it so he could look at his forearm. "Got more done?"

Sloane glanced down, blinking in confusion before nodding. "Oh, yeah, just some shading."

Sloane's entire left arm was a canvas of ink. Dean had alternated between watching the tapestry of tattoos spread across his friend's arm to not seeing Sloane for days or weeks at a time and being surprised by the sudden appearance of another one. Sloane wasn't a man for symbols, so most of his tattoos were animals, snakes twined around the barrel of a firing gun, tigers leaping from the depths of vibrant flames, and a huge hawk materializing from thick clouds of smoke. Just about any majestic predator Dean could think of was there, starting just above Sloane's wrist and working their way up his arm and over his shoulder.

"You've run out of arm," Dean noted.

"That's why I got another one."

"Mmm, and yet you elected to go over your chest," Dean pointed out.

"I mean, there's space there, it works," Sloane said.

Dean chuckled, shaking his head as he pressed his fingers to Sloane's wrist and counted. He didn't need to track the clock's second hand over the bed, but he watched it anyway to be more precise than simply making a trained guess. Sloane remained still as Dean pressed his fingers beneath the man's defined jaw, opened for Dean to inspect his mouth and throat, and allowed himself to be carefully manhandled while Dean checked him over.

"Is this exam part of the list they love so much?" Sloane asked.

Dean laughed softly, listening to Sloane's breathing. "You know it."

Sloane rolled his eyes, waiting until Dean was done before speaking again. "Doesn't inspire confidence, though, does it?"

Dean looked up, bemused. "How so?"

"Well, if their whole thing is ensuring we eat right and do our workouts, why the constant checkups?"

Dean chuckled. "Because General Winter loves his lists more than anyone, and he wants to make sure everyone is healthy."

Admittedly, Dean wondered about the checkups, which were required more often than Dean thought necessary. Then again, without the frequent checkups, he wouldn't have caught the first sign of melanoma on a captain a couple of months back.

"General Winter is just cautious," Dean continued.

"Some might call that paranoid," Sloane said with a grin.

Dean smirked. "Some, huh? Someone like you?"

"I would never have such an unkind thought about our General."

"Just like you wouldn't eat the last of my ice cream I accidentally left in your freezer," Dean snorted.

"I'm telling you, there's a thief on this base who's out for nothing but ice cream...and cookies."

Dean looked up, eyes widening. "You're the one who ate the bag of cookies off my counter? I thought I did a bit of sleepwalking or night eating and didn't remember."

"I have no idea what you're talking about," Sloane said in what Dean thought was the fakest of innocent voices.

Dean scowled. "You're a shit. I'm going to put your charts back and try to forget you're a dirty dessert thief. Get dressed, you animal."

Sloane's chuckle followed him out of the room. "Yeah, but I'm your animal."

Didn't Dean wish that were true?

Sloane had dressed by the time he returned, and only the slightest flicker of regret entered the back of Dean's mind when he saw. It was gone just like that, and he held out his hand again to take Sloane's arm.

Dean looked him over. "Just come off a double?"

"Shows, huh?"

"A bit, yeah."

Sloane didn't bat an eye when the needle drove beneath his skin. "Yeah, stuck with a jackass all night, too."

"You always say that. Simmons?"

"Yeah. Jackass."

Dean chuckled. "Going back to sleep, then?"

Sloane nodded. "I'll get a few hours in, but then I've got the night to myself. You?"

"If you can believe it, this will be my second day in a row with a normal, single shift."

Sloane snorted. "A miracle. Doing anything tonight?"

"Mmm, wild orgy."

Sloane smirked. "Get all your slots filled?"

"That's kind of the point of an orgy."

"Alright, smartass."

Dean grinned, capping the injector. "No, got nothing to do, why?"

"Maybe come on over, and we can watch some shitty action movie, drink beers and chill?"

It had been a while since their last movie night. It was almost exactly as Sloane had detailed. The two of them found some movie, usually a bad one, and sat around, drinking beers idly and spending time together. The ritual had begun when the two of them had been on watch together, staring up at the sky and talking about their lives. When they'd graduated, it had become nights spent in the barracks, playing cards and talking. Now that they had their respective places, they could spend actual alone time together, doing absolutely nothing.

And they were the highlight of Dean's week.

Dean winked, going to dispose of the injector. "It's a date."

SLOANE

Shuffling about in the small space that made up his kitchen, Sloane grabbed the hamburger buns. As the patties sizzled away in the pan, he unwound the plastic bag and pulled out a few buns to spread a thin layer of butter inside each. With that done, he dropped them in the other heated pan.

He looked up at the sound of his door opening but didn't bother to check. Only a few people had a key to his apartment, and only one would walk in unannounced.

"Christ, that smells delicious," Dean called, followed by the thump of his shoes being kicked off.

Sloane sighed. "Put them—"

"On the shoe rack, I know, I know," Dean grumbled.

Sloane chuckled as he listened to Dean mutter under his breath. Having grown up in small, close quarters with three other people, Sloane learned early on how important it was to keep everything tidy and organized. The less space used up, the more room there was, and that tidiness had been ingrained even further into his personality by the rigors of basic training and then military life. Dean, however, was considerably more lax. While the man was meticulous and attentive to detail in his work, in his casual life, Dean left clean laundry in a basket for a week straight, and his kitchen drawers were organized in a way that made sense only to him.

Dean stomped into view, shaking a damp lock of blond hair free from his forehead. "Again, I say, that smells delicious."

Sloane glanced at him. "Raining?"

"It was just a sprinkle at first, and then it decided to piss all over me, which was great."

Sloane snorted, plucking the toasted buns from the pan and laying them on plates. "You know where the towels are."

"Yeah, I'm not listening if I get your couch wet," Dean huffed, turning and stomping off.

Sloane shook his head as the man, who probably didn't weigh more than 160lbs, somehow managed to make enough noise for someone twice his size. While Sloane had never worked alongside Dean in the field during their almost simultaneous deployment, he knew Dean could move with grace and great stealth. Yet, take him out of the field and put him in a casual setting, and the man stomped around like an ogre.

As Sloane dropped the burgers onto the buns and grabbed the bag of chips, Dean reappeared. During the few times Dean had been over and used one of his towels, the sight always amused Sloane. Due to his size, Sloane bought the biggest and usually fluffiest towels he could find. They suited him, but on someone of Dean's stature, they looked like blankets wrapped around him, or in this case, a cape that started as a cowl.

Dean rubbed at his head vigorously. "I'm surprised they haven't yelled at me for my hair yet."

Sloane raised a brow. "I keep meaning to ask you who

you're bribing to let your hair grow more than a few inches, let alone longer."

Dean shrugged. "I keep forgetting, and no one has corrected me yet. I think I'm the only guy on base with actual hair instead of just a suggestion."

"A suggestion, huh?"

"I mean, it's better than saying everyone else is wandering around with nothing more than peach fuzz," Dean said.

Sloane held out one of the plates. "That's pretty heavy criticism coming from you. Especially since I distinctly remember a certain drunk medic telling me how he got into the military because he *really* liked men in uniform."

Dean hummed, curling his lip as he took the plate. "You're not going to let me live that night down, are you?"

"Not so long as I still have a functioning memory and mouth," Sloane said with a grin.

"Well, I guess I have no choice but to find a way to stop one or both of those things," Dean said.

Despite his smaller frame, Dean had a surprisingly strong tolerance to alcohol. In the few years Sloane had known the man, he could count the number of times he'd seen Dean more than buzzed on both hands, and he'd only seen him wasted once. Sloane suspected it had only been the one time because that night had been so full of stories with which Sloane loved to regale him. Well, and some part of him wondered if perhaps Dean just hated the idea of Sloane seeming like that too.

"And then I asked you how you manage to get through a normal day if you like men in uniform so much," Sloane continued.

Dean sighed, turning to walk away. "I hate you."

"And you said—"

"Hate, hate, hate!"

"Like a good little private, you stand at attention all day."

"Hate."

Sloane trailed behind Dean, still chuckling as they entered the living room. The apartment was the first place Sloane had ever been able to call his own. On most bases, he probably would have been out of luck finding a place on-site. There were typically more soldiers than living spaces, and generally, those homes went to married servicemen. Fort Dale, however, wasn't a densely populated base and possessed not just homes but apartments for its soldiers. There was enough space for Sloane to snatch one up with little problem, save for all the tedious paperwork.

The only downside for Sloane was that the place wasn't all that large. Not that Sloane had a lot of things, but for someone his size, small spaces felt confining. Especially when he had to invest in a huge armchair and couch combo to be comfortable. His bedroom was no different, with most of the room taken up by a huge bed, for which he'd paid good money. Sloane hadn't bothered with decorating much. A few pictures of his family lay scattered about, and a few posters of movies and sports teams he liked. The main focus in the living room was the huge TV and sound system, which he'd spent a great deal of money on so he could enjoy his time at home.

And, well, he thought it added to the movie and game nights he and Dean shared.

Dean flopped down on the couch, forced to scramble as his plate almost tipped up. Just as Dean was graceful and focused on the job, he was lurching and clumsy when he wasn't working. It was a strange dichotomy that most people didn't get to see. Sloane wasn't sure Dean was even aware of it, but his friend's true personality didn't show itself until he was comfortable and away from prying eyes.

"Please don't spill shit on my cushions," Sloane said, easing himself onto the couch with more grace.

I'M STRAIGHT, RIGHT?

Dean held the plate out. "Not a single crumb or drop of grease has left the plate, see?"

Sloane ignored him, powering up the TV. "You heard me."

"I forgot to grab beer," Dean told him.

Sloane shrugged, cycling through the movie list. "There's a few in the fridge if you want some, but I'm not worried about it."

He didn't need alcohol to get through their nights. The two of them had always gotten along great, starting from the first conversation when they'd been put on watch together. Sloane had first spoken as they sat, staring out into the dark woods as the hours ticked away. Sloane could still remember the apprehensive look on Dean's face as he eyed Sloane and the careful way he'd replied. Not the greatest start, but Sloane had pretended not to notice and continued chatting.

"Hello? Sloane?"

He blinked, turning to look at Dean. "What?"

Dean frowned. "You okay?"

"Yeah, I was...thinking."

"Don't hurt yourself."

Sloane smacked Dean's leg with the remote. "I was remembering the first time we talked, asshole."

Dean snorted, rubbing the spot where he'd been struck. "God, I thought you would end up being the world's biggest asshole."

"Everyone does. It's just my wonderful personality showing through."

Dean chuckled. "I mean, you can be a grumpy dick, but you weren't that night. You asked if I was used to cold nights because you remembered I was from Arizona."

Sloane shrugged. "It was the first thing to pop into my head."

"It was probably one of the best things you could have asked. You never said anything during downtime, so I figured you didn't give a shit about any of us. Kind of surprised me you remembered where I was from," Dean said.

"I paid attention," Sloane protested.

Maybe not to most things, but Dean had caught his eye from the first time they'd had a moment to breathe. There was something infectious about the way Dean laughed, and even when they were sore all over and worn to the bone, Dean still found a reason to smile. Dean didn't bitch and whine like some of the other recruits had, and despite being on the smaller side, had worked just as hard, sometimes even harder, during the more strength-oriented demands on them.

"You looked cold," Sloane continued.

Dean smiled. "And I thought you were a little lonely."

There was that. After living his whole life in cramped quarters with two sisters and an energetic mother, Sloane had grown used to noise and chatter. Most of their fellow recruits were just as chatty, but they tended to give him a wide berth, though his dour attitude probably hadn't encouraged them to change their thinking. It hadn't been until he'd been left alone with Dean that Sloane had found a reason to reach out and have a little more human interaction.

And so, the greatest friendship Sloane had ever had was born.

Dean's eyes lit up, pointing at the screen. "Ooh, that one!"

"Seriously?" Sloane asked as he looked over the preview flashing on the screen.

"It looks amazing!"

"It looks like garbage."

"Amazing garbage."

Shaking his head, Sloane hit the play button and let the movie start. There was no arguing with Dean when he got excited, and Sloane didn't see any harm in letting him have his way.

* * *

SLOANE SHOULD HAVE KNOWN Dean wouldn't make it through the entire movie. Dean worked a lot of hours in the clinic, but Sloane knew his friend didn't sleep that well when he finally caught a few hours. Dean was tight-lipped about what caused his frequent sleep problems, and Sloane knew better than to push him.

Which was why, as the second movie started, Dean had shifted from sitting on the couch to lying on it. Dean sprawled along the length of the couch with his head on Sloane's leg, making himself comfortable. It was a position they found themselves in frequently, and Sloane slung an arm over Dean without a second thought.

Halfway through the second movie, Dean snoozed soundly, his chest rising and falling with deep, even breaths. Whatever demons haunted Dean's sleep, they didn't follow him whenever he came to rest at Sloane's.

Maybe that was why Dean slept over so often.

So, Sloane finished the rest of the movie with Dean sleeping peacefully, head in his lap. Anyone who looked at the movie he was watching might have thought it'd been Sloane's choice. A beautiful woman with a considerable chest and a penchant for tight clothing swung her way from fight to fight, taking down scores of men who far outweighed her. But no, the decision had been all Dean's, the man's love of ass-kicking women in action movies showing itself again. Sloane wasn't a fan, but it was flashy and entertaining enough to hold his interest.

In truth, he wasn't paying attention to what was happening on the screen. Despite his statement about not caring about the beer, Sloane had dipped into the supply he had stowed away and let it work its magic. By the time he'd worked through a third, he was pleasantly warm and filled with a lassitude that had him half-dozing.

Dean continued to sleep peacefully through the next movie, which had started to auto-play. Sloane sat, peacefully reclining against the back of the couch, his eyes half-closed. Dean's head on his leg was a comforting pressure, and Sloane ran his thumb in small circles over the sleeping man's shoulder. Whether they were simply existing close to one another, talking, or doing their own thing in the same room, Sloane always enjoyed their time together.

Dean stirred, turning his face into Sloane's thigh and inhaling sharply. Sloane looked down, watching his friend as he waited to see how Dean would wake up. When Dean looked up at him, eyes blurry from sleep, Sloane let himself relax.

"How long have I been out?" Dean asked.

"Mmm, about an hour, hour and a half," Sloane told him.

Dean groaned, flopping his arm onto the couch. "Damn it."

"You always sleep like a rock when you're here," Sloane chuckled.

"Ugh, I know. Just wish it didn't happen in the middle of the evening. Now I'll never get to sleep later."

"You can always crash here."

Dean blinked slowly, shrugging. "Yeah, probably should, huh?"

Neither moved as Dean slowly brought himself back to the world of the waking. Along with their close friendship came a closeness on a physical level that Sloane had never questioned. A few people had seen the ease of the contact between the two men and questioned it, but Sloane had always shrugged it off.

It didn't make a difference to Sloane that Dean was gay. For him, having someone he could feel comfortable enough with just simply touching was nice. His family had always been extremely affectionate growing up, and while Sloane was considered reserved by their standards, he still missed human contact. With Dean, that sort of contact came easily, and neither of them made a fuss over it.

Dean grunted, pushing himself up into a sitting position and stretched. Sloane watched him, noting that he looked more rested than before. He suspected it would take more than an hour's nap to get Dean back to full force, but he also knew there was no point in mentioning it. As warm and happy as Dean was, the man could be pretty cranky if he thought someone was trying to mother him, never realizing the irony.

"There any chips left?" Dean asked, standing up.

"Half a bag," Sloane said.

"More than enough."

When Dean returned, he plopped himself back on the couch, lying on his side again. This time, he didn't lay his head in Sloane's lap, but he did curl up against him, open bag of chips in hand as he munched away happily.

"You look like a raccoon," Sloane observed.

Dean looked up, pausing with the chips between his fingers and halfway to his mouth. "What?"

Sloane snorted, shaking his head. "Continue foraging."

Dean frowned, popping the chips into his mouth. "Jerk."

Sloane flopped an arm over him. "Yeah, and you're stuck with me."

DEAN

Groaning, Dean fumbled for the buzzing phone he'd set on the table the night before. He'd slept on Sloane's couch enough times that he could find the insistent device with one swipe of his hand and bring it to his face. With an annoyed huff, he turned the alarm off, wishing he could get a few more winks in before he had to get up.

Still grumbling, he heaved himself off the couch before he convinced himself he could rest his eyes a bit more. No matter how much the military had drilled a sense of urgency and alertness into him in the field, he'd never entirely managed to hold to it in his daily life. The 'one more minute' game was one he never won, and Dean knew better than to risk it again.

Stumbling into the kitchen, he went directly to the coffee maker. Flipping the top, he smiled as his eyes rested on the coffee grounds. Only a deeply ingrained habit had driven him to open the appliance in the first place. Sloane had prepared the coffee maker, as he always did, whether Dean was staying with him or Sloane was staying with Dean. The only reason the man hadn't set it to pre-brew was Sloane hadn't known when Dean would wake up.

Still smiling, Dean pressed the brew button and let it gurgle away as he went to the fridge. Sometimes, it was easy to forget how well Sloane knew him. Down to the finest detail, Sloane could predict him. He even placed Dean's favored brand of bottled water at the front, among the ones Sloane typically bought for himself.

His smile turned down a little as he snagged the bottle, cracking it open. It was easy to forget, yet it was the hardest thing for Dean to acknowledge. To see it was to witness just how easily the two of them clicked and how well they could mesh. Change just one little thing, and maybe the two of them—

Dean shook his head, tipping the bottle and downing the ice-cold contents. Sloane might prefer his water a little warmer than freezing when he woke up, but Dean had always been fond of ice-cold water in the morning. Along with the dose of caffeine, it went a long way toward making him feel human.

Sadly, the water wasn't enough, and Dean always hated waiting for the coffee to finish brewing. Before he could grow too annoyed, however, a blinking light caught his eye. Dean turned toward it, realizing Sloane had left his phone plugged in on the kitchen counter. Sloane never needed an alarm to get up, something Dean considered inhuman.

Curiosity got the better of him, and he tapped a button on the phone, bringing the screen to life. Sloane had never bothered to put a password on his phone, betting that there wouldn't be many people willing to get close enough to take his phone, and so far, he'd been right. The messages from Sloane's sisters and two from his mother were sitting on the screen, though Dean only read the names before turning the screen off again.

Dean supposed it would be all too easy to be jealous of the family Sloane had. The four of them were incredibly close, and for all his bitching about having to text his sisters daily, Sloane did it without hesitation. Dean couldn't even remember the last time his parents bothered to check on him, and then again, he hadn't attempted to reach out to them either.

Pouring himself a cup of coffee, he mused on the strangeness of his childhood. His parents hadn't abused him, and they made sure all his needs were met, and if he wanted something, so long as it was within reason, he was given it. Where Sloane's mother had struggled to feed and clothe her three children, Dean's own and his father had given Dean anything he'd ever wanted.

Yet, there was always something missing. A rift Dean could never explain, and the few times he'd tried to cross the divide, it had been like attempting to mount an expedition through the snowy tundra. Too many unknown landmarks, and the land, while not overtly hostile, offered no comfort. Dean learned a long time ago that his parents simply...were.

"How long you been at that pot?"

Dean stiffened, whirling around with his coffee cup clenched in his grip. Mid-spin, his mind registered the familiar rumble of Sloane's voice, but he didn't recover enough to save the coffee from sloshing all over the floor. Dean hissed, dancing back as the hot coffee splashed his bare feet.

"Shit. Sorry," Dean muttered.

Sloane blinked slowly, eyes on Dean's face. "You okay?"

Dean shook his scalded foot. "I'm fine, just a little hot coffee, I'll live."

Sloane continued to stare, and Dean realized Sloane hadn't been asking about the coffee. Dean's fingers renewed their tight grip, knuckles turning white before he forced himself to relax. With difficulty, he turned his gaze away from Sloane's, not wanting his friend to see something in his eyes. Bad enough that his reaction to such a benign surprise had been too sharp and quick, Dean didn't want to face his haunted memories.

He did that enough in his dreams.

Fumbling with one of the drawers, Dean pulled out a towel, crouching to clean up the mess. While he and Sloane had been deployed to the same desolate stretch of rocks and sand, they had been assigned to different units. Dean had found himself loaned out to a special tactics group and had been forced to keep his mouth shut whenever he and Sloane ran into one another in the field. Sloane's deployment had ended a few months before Dean's, and fittingly, that was when everything had gone to hell.

Dean looked up from the floor and winced when he saw Sloane still looking down at him. Sloane knew something had happened in the few months after they'd last seen one another, but Dean had kept his peace. Sloane thought Dean was respecting his orders to keep his mouth shut, which boiled down to feelings that Dean didn't trust him.

Clearing his throat, Dean wrung the towel out in the sink. "There's more than enough in the pot for you to have some if you want."

Sloane grunted, stepping around the counter to retrieve a cup from the cabinet overhead. Dean rinsed the towel out, letting the pleasant, mundane sounds of running water and the gurgle of coffee poured into a mug wash over him. The sounds and smells of a normal life, where he was safe, where death wasn't lurking around every corner, were far more pleasant than the memories pushing at the edges of his mind.

A presence pushed itself up behind him, and Dean stiffened in surprise. The lingering scent of Sloane's woodsy cologne filled his nostrils, and the tension in Dean's shoulders eased. Sloane pressed his forehead against the side of Dean's head and held it there. They said nothing as Dean stood at the sink with a wet rag in his hand, soaking in the warmth and comfort of his friend.

Taking a deep breath, Sloane stepped away. "How much time do you have?"

Dean flipped the faucet off, squeezing the rag. "I'm doing alright."

"What? No rushing off because you're going to be late?" Sloane asked wryly.

Dean turned, swatting Sloane lazily with the towel. "Quit."

Sloane wrinkled his nose, wiping at the damp spot on his hip. "You're the one who can't keep track of time."

"I do just fine." Dean sniffed as he set the rag over the faucet.

"Only because you've kept working out," Sloane said with a sip of his coffee.

Dean refilled his cup. "I like to think the occasional morning rush is as good at waking me up as drinking a whole pot of coffee."

Sloane eyed him over the rim of his cup for a moment longer before reaching down and picking up his phone. Dean watched him quietly, only then becoming aware of Sloane's state. Though his hair was too short to be disheveled, Sloane looked sleepy-eyed, with thick stubble on his jaw, and his voice was still rough from having just woken up. He hadn't bothered to do more than throw on a pair of shorts before stepping into the kitchen.

Still sleepy and a little raw from his overreaction, Dean scanned Sloane's body as the man tapped away at his phone. Sloane was just as fastidious about keeping up with his workout routine as Dean, though the results were more obvious. Sloane's chest was solid muscle, and his stomach was flat, with the faintest hint of sculpted lines. It didn't help that Sloane's body had a healthy layer of dark hair, just enough to send Dean's heart racing with anticipation but not so much that he couldn't see the skin beneath it.

Sloane chuckled. "And just like that, she's onto the next."

Dean jerked guiltily. "What?"

"Shawna. She was losing her mind over some boy the other day, and now she's telling me about some new boy she met while watching a movie with friends."

Dean focused his attention on Sloane's face, snorting. "What did you expect? She could never focus on anything for too long. Remember her salsa lessons?"

Sloane rolled his eyes. "Yoga."

"Meditation."

"Knitting."

"Photography."

Sloane sighed. "Nothing will compare to when she decided to take up tap dancing. That was before I shipped out for basic, and I don't think my mom has managed to get the scuffs out of the floor since."

Dean laughed. "My mother would have had a fit if I tried to do something like that."

"That because it was a girl thing to do, or because you would've ruined her floors?"

"The latter. She never really gave a shit when she found out I was gay. My father said something about how that was the 'college' thing to do and then just shrugged when I reminded him I was going into the service."

"They're probably betting you'll get out and go to school."

Dean shrugged. "Probably, but I've already renewed once, and I don't see any reason not to again."

Sloane cocked his head. "You've never talked about what you wanted to do after serving. I guess I figured you'd decided on staying."

"I hadn't...made up my mind, actually. Honestly, when I renewed, it was because I didn't know what I wanted to do if I were to get out. Go to college? And do what? Nothing called to me. There wasn't any one thing I was good at."

"I think being a Doc counts for a lot on the civilian side of the world."

Dean snorted. "And do what? The same thing I've been doing here? What's the point of leaving then? It might not seem like much to my parents or people like them, but hell, at least here, I have a purpose. I have direction. If I left, all I'd do is wander around, unsure what to do with myself."

"You stay because it gives you meaning," Sloane said simply.

"Not the most thrilling of reasons," Dean admitted as he refueled his cup.

"When the fuck did a reason have to be thrilling? If it's a reason that works for you, then fuck it, go with it. If you being in the military gives you what you need, keep the contract going and make a life of it. If you find out you don't want to do it anymore, stop after it expires and don't renew. Simple."

Dean chuckled, sipping his coffee and nodding. Dean wasn't sure if Sloane tended to cut to the heart of a problem because he was hardwired that way or because he'd been forced to after helping raise his two admittedly emotional and melodramatic sisters.

"You haven't exactly talked about what you were going to do other than this stuff," Dean pointed out.

Sloane shrugged. "I might stick with it, but eh, probably not. Military can always use more grunts, but I don't want to be a grunt forever. Maybe I'll find something with the cops, wouldn't that be something? Poor kid growing up to be a soldier, then a cop, that would get them talking back home."

Dean grinned. "Probably no more than my parents' friends."

Sloane blinked. "I mean, my neighborhood is filled with nothing but druggies, gangsters, and burnouts. What the hell would people in a nice neighborhood have to talk shit about?"

They had grown up on opposite sides of the proverbial tracks. Sloane had grown up with people being shot on his street, muggings in the alley next to his apartment, and drug dealers lurking on every corner. It had always puzzled Sloane when he was given a peek into the troubles of upper-middle-class America.

Dean sighed. "Our neighbor's daughter was in med school before I left, and their son was on his way to valedictorian of his graduating year. Across the street were twins whose science project caught international scientific interest, something about cleaning up plastics in the ocean. One of my cousins just got accepted to some big law firm in New York, and another is this big nature photographer who even got into National Geographic."

Sloane frowned. "And? Is this one of those things where your parents think something stupid?"

Dean laughed. "Compared to all those examples, how would I stand up? I did alright in school, never was part of a club of any mention, and after graduation, I signed up for the military. My parents thought it was just a phase, that I was going through a 'rebel' stage, their words, not mine, and that I would work it out."

Sloane squinted. "Signing up to serve the government...to go fight and maybe die in some part of the world...is a...rebel stage?"

"Yep."

"That's the stupidest fucking thing I've ever heard."

"Only because you haven't been at one of their family dinners. That's where the really fun things are said."

Sloane shook his head. "I swear, everything I hear about your parents makes me want to hit them upside the head."

Dean shrugged. "That's just how things work in my family and with their social circle."

"They should appreciate the son they have, not try to make him into something they think he should be."

Dean smiled, touched. "You clearly don't know how things work in middle-class suburbia."

"And I don't want to either, sounds stupid."

"Only because you have a family who likes you."

Sloane raised a brow. "They liked you too."

Dean paused and then let out an exasperated sigh at Sloane's grin. "Please. Do not."

"Shawna, especially," Sloane continued.

Dean pointed. "No."

"Mom said she was heartbroken after she told her you were never going to be interested in her, and not just because she's like, ten years younger than you."

"At least I stopped you from telling her," Dean said, remembering the previous Easter when they'd both been given leave and had flown to visit Sloane's family.

"I still think it would have been funny if I had."

Sloane's version of funny was likely a lot different from Shawna's. Despite loving his time around such a vibrant and warm family, Dean hadn't been blind to the teenage girl's flirtations with him. Everyone else had been aware of Shawna's feelings, but unlike Dean, Sloane and his mother had found it absolutely hilarious. It had certainly made Easter dinner more awkward, but Dean still counted it as the best Easter he'd ever had.

Dean rinsed his cup out. "And would you look at the time? Suddenly, I realize I have to go on shift."

Sloane chuckled, leaning against the counter behind him with the smuggest expression possible. "How convenient."

Dean ignored him, mainly because the sight of Sloane, cocky and sprawled out, was incredibly distracting. He shifted his attention to his neatly folded pile of clothes next to the couch and scooped them up. Dean could feel Sloane's eyes on him the whole time, and he repressed the urge to look again. He knew from experience how easy it was to fall into feasting on the sight of Sloane looking impossibly handsome and casually sexy.

"You can run, but you can't hide," Sloane called after him.

"Tell me something I don't know," Dean muttered as he closed the bathroom door behind him.

SLOANE

Unable to help himself, Sloane watched the clock above the door to the guardhouse. Technology might have grown by leaps and bounds, but the military still insisted on using the cheapest things possible. That included an analog clock that monotonously ticked away in the silence.

Not that silence was easy to come by.

"I'm just saying, why take the drink and not even talk to me?" Simmons complained.

"Not her fault you're dumb enough to buy her a drink without asking. You ask me, you're the dumbass who got played, suck it up," Trisha said.

"Least she could have done was shoot me down and give me the drink back."

"Free booze."

"Rude is what it is."

Sloane rolled his eyes. "Have you considered that maybe your oh-so-stunning personality scared her off?"

"I didn't even get a chance to say anything!"

Trisha chuckled. "Which is the smartest thing she could have done."

I'M STRAIGHT, RIGHT?

"You guys are no help."

Sloane snorted. "I don't have the patience to help you with your fuck ups, and I definitely don't want to. Try acting like a normal fucking person when you're around a good-looking woman for once, maybe that'll help."

Trisha eyed him. "What happened to not helping him?"

Sloane ignored her. "And while you're at it, act like a normal fucking person when you're around us too. That would be nice."

"We both know that's not happening anytime soon," Trisha said.

Simmons crossed his arms, slumping into his seat. "You guys suck."

Sloane glanced at the clock, smiling. "Yeah, but only for you."

"Why are you so happy?" Trisha asked.

Sloane nodded his head toward the clock. "That's the end for me. I'll leave you to deal with his pouting ass while I get the next couple of days for pure freedom."

"Oh, great, thanks. You get his bottom lip jutting out, and now I get to deal with the fallout."

"As if he wasn't going to do it anyway after getting shot down again."

"I'm right here!" Simmons protested.

"We know," Sloane and Trisha said in unison.

Their response had Simmons slouching in his seat even further and widening Sloane's grin. He shot Trisha a wink, who returned the gesture with her tongue sticking out, and Sloane pushed out of his seat. He wasn't often able to get more than a day off, and he had every intention of taking advantage of it.

Stepping out into the late afternoon air, he took a deep breath and grinned. Sloane knew Dean also had the next day off, and he wanted to do something with his friend. Dean's sleepover the night before had been fun, but it had left Sloane uncomfortable and a little frustrated.

There was clearly something wrong with Dean. Sloane didn't know what had happened after he'd returned to the States, but clearly, it was eating away at Dean. Sloane could only hope it was that Dean was sworn to secrecy, but his gut told him it was more. For all his casualness and typical lack of inhibition in expressing himself, Dean could be incredibly stubborn about certain things. It was all too easy for Sloane to see Dean keeping something to himself out of some misguided desire to work through it on his own.

Sloane would worry about that another time. First things first, he needed to do a bit of shopping. His groceries were a little sparse, and he wanted to see if he could coax Dean over to his apartment on their shared day off. As much as Sloane would like to drag the story out of Dean, he knew Dean would talk if and when he wanted to, no sooner, no later. What Sloane could do, however, was create a place and time where Dean could relax and not have to jump all over the place.

Nodding to himself, he began walking back to his apartment to clean off and change. Despite Dean getting off shift in a couple of hours, he hadn't said anything to Sloane about doing something the following day. Sloane took that as a sign that Dean wanted to do something on his own and resolved to send him a text later to ask if he'd be down for another chill-out night tomorrow.

But first, he needed to do some shopping in town.

* * *

SLOANE HUFFED as another person nearly collided with him on the sidewalk. He'd forgotten it was Friday, and the tourist town of Dalton, a short drive from Fort Dale, was crowded.

Worse, he had taken longer than intended to get ready, and with twilight turning into night, the streets were even more packed than usual. While he was trying to keep his bags of groceries close before they were torn free, everyone else was ready to start a long night of fun.

For a moment, Sloane considered taking his groceries home and returning to town. It had been a while since he'd last gone out and had a night to himself. Before he'd been deployed, there had been several nights where he'd go out on the town and find out what sort of trouble he could get into. Simmons might have commented out of exasperation, but he'd been partially right. Sloane's bed had been shared several times.

However, that all changed when he returned to the States. Sure, there was still the occasional fling here and there, but as Sloane slipped from his early to mid-twenties, he'd discovered he had less of a taste for it. Honestly, it was easier and far more fun to enjoy some of his free time alone and the rest with his best friend. And hell, if he ever felt the urge to scratch that particular itch, he wouldn't have to go far with the town so close.

Lost in his thoughts, Sloane found his car parked alongside a meter. There was still plenty of time on it, and he figured someone else would praise their good fortune when they inevitably took his vacant space. With relief, he shoved the grocery bags into the back seat, closed the door, and prepared to climb into the driver's seat.

He paused as a familiar laugh nearby brought his head up. Turning to look for the source, it took a minute before he spotted a familiar face in the crowd. Sloane cocked his head as he watched Dean walk through the sea of people, grinning ear to ear. Dean wasn't usually the type to go out on the town, preferring to stay in the barracks whenever Sloane decided to have some fun. Sloane had clocked it up to his friend being a bit of a 'shut away,' but as it turned out, Dean liked to go out.

Sloane made to raise his hand to see if he could catch Dean's attention and froze as someone jogged up to Dean. There was something in the strange man's hand, and he shoved it into Dean's grip with an ear-to-ear grin. Dean let out another laugh, goofy and playful, as he looked down at what he'd been given, shaking his head in disbelief. Sloane's eyes widened as he watched the man bend forward, stealing a kiss from Dean, which earned him a quieter and far more private laugh.

Some distant part of his mind was sure he looked ridiculous, but Sloane couldn't help ogling the two men. It was obvious that not only was Dean on a date, but their casual air told Sloane it wasn't the first or even the second. Dean had always been quiet about what he did in his spare time, and Sloane had never thought to question it. As he watched Dean nudge the man, slipping an arm through his, Sloane remembered how much quieter Dean had been lately.

He stared at the two of them as they walked along the opposite sidewalk. That was until Dean happened to glance Sloane's way. The way his friend's eyes drifted over him, only to snap back with eye-widening recognition, might have been funny in any other context. As it was, he could only return Dean's gaze, slowly tilting his head to one side as he tried to process what he was seeing.

Dean's date noticed something was wrong, turning to speak softly to Dean. Dean licked his lips nervously, nodding in Sloane's direction, bringing the date's attention to him. For a few seconds, the three of them gazed at one another across the street, no one sure what to do. Finally, Dean's unknown date shook himself out of it and, with a gentle pull on Dean's wrist, led him over to Sloane.

"Hi, Sloane," Dean began quietly, his voice almost lost in the drone around them.

"Dean," Sloane said.

Dean glanced at the other man. "This is Marco."

Now they were closer, Sloane could make out the finer details of Dean's date. Objectively speaking, Sloane would give Dean credit, as he had caught an attractive man. Marco was taller than Dean but stood a few inches shorter than Sloane. He had strong features, with an angular, cut jaw accented by the lightest peppering of dark stubble. Marco obviously took care of himself, the forearms sticking out from his shirt were toned with muscle. Though a little messy, his dark brown hair was well-kept and bright, intelligent hazel eyes looked up at Sloane warily but without fear.

"Good to finally meet you," Marco said in a rich baritone as he held out his hand.

Sloane's eyes snapped back to Dean. "Oh, so *you've* heard of *me*."

Dean winced. "Sloane."

Sloane took Marco's hand, gripping it tightly and giving it a single shake. "Nice to meet you. Just found out you existed, but hey, nice to meet you anyway."

"It was...I planned on telling you," Dean said.

Sloane looked at Marco. "This whole keeping it a secret thing, your idea?"

Marco shook his head. "It wasn't our intention to keep anything a secret."

"Mmm, and yet, here it is, a secret."

Sloane could see Dean cringing hard enough it was a miracle the man didn't retreat into his chest cavity. Guilt pinged in Sloane's heart, and he hated himself for bringing a look of shame to Dean's face. But damn it, why would Dean keep something like this from Sloane? Did he think Sloane wouldn't like it? Did he think Sloane would be a dick to Marco?

"It was...just us trying to be sure," Marco continued.

Sure of what? That Sloane would be able to handle the news? That Sloane wouldn't be able to argue with Dean having finally found himself a man because they'd gone on several dates?

"I'm sorry, Sloane. It wasn't supposed to be a secret, I promise," Dean said quietly.

The guilt deepened, and Sloane opened his mouth. Whether to tell Dean he'd get over it or to ask for further clarification, he wasn't sure. What he did know was Marco had slid an arm behind Dean's back to comfort him. Sloane pressed his lips into a thin line, refusing to let any words escape as he watched Marco gaze down at Dean, his expression hidden from Sloane's view.

Wasn't it bad enough that Sloane had to find out by accident that his best friend had been keeping a relationship from him? Did the guy really have to do the whole boyfriend thing right in front of Sloane while he was still processing that there even was a boyfriend? Sloane didn't give a shit that it was two guys in front of him doing it. What bothered him was the complete lack of taste.

"So, how'd you meet? Random? Find each other in the bar?" Sloane asked, hearing the anger in his voice and unable to quell it.

"App," Marco said, squeezing Dean.

Sloane turned his burning gaze toward Marco. "And what do you do, Marco?"

"IT for a local tech company," Marco said, holding Sloane's gaze easily.

Sloane nodded jerkily. "Oh, I see. Fancy. Perfect if you ever have to take him home, eh, Dean?"

Dean's head snapped up, eyes sparking. "Sloane, what the hell?"

Not that Dean had ever cared about that sort of thing, and Sloane didn't know why he'd even felt the need to bring it up. It honestly didn't matter if Dean chose to date someone with a high-end college degree or a blue-collar construction worker, Sloane wouldn't have cared one way or another. What ate at him, what drove the indignant, willful anger, was that Dean had kept this from him.

Sloane could accept that Dean wouldn't talk about what had happened to him out in the field. He could accept that Dean would keep his fevered nightmares to himself and never do more than apologize for his occasional overreaction to what were, at the end of the day, simply minor scares. What he couldn't accept was that Dean thought it right to keep his budding relationship with someone a secret from Sloane. They were supposed to be best friends. They were supposed to share almost everything, especially something that should have been wonderful and worth celebrating.

And *God*, why wouldn't Marco stop touching Dean, just for ten fucking seconds?

"I worked pretty hard for it, but I wouldn't call it fancy," Marco answered in his infuriatingly calm voice.

"And got yourself a military man. Shit, you guys could get married now, get yourself even nicer housing if you wanted," Sloane continued in a voice that was both seething and oddly cheerful.

"I *hope* I have myself a good man. Whether I do or not remains to be seen," Marco said while Dean stared in dumbfounded shock beside him.

Sloane's brow rose in polite surprise that he didn't feel. "Oh? Hasn't committed, has he? He's a wily one. Better keep an eye on him before he finds someone else."

Marco tilted his head, scoffing slightly. "I think...I should go. I don't think I'm...helping by being here."

Dean snapped out of his stupor, reaching out to take hold of Marco with a curt shake of his head. "No, you stay. Sloane, I think you're the one who needs to go."

Sloane didn't blame him. "Me? I'm just trying to get some answers and figure out everything I've missed out on."

Dean's jaw tightened. "You're being an ass. I'm sorry I didn't tell you immediately, but this is beyond stupid. Go home and let me enjoy my night."

Sloane wanted to argue, demand answers from Dean, and yank the man away from Marco's grip. Instead, he gave a low huff before all but ripping the driver's side door to his car off the hinges in his effort to open it. He was just as brutal in slamming it and rocking the frame, and he swore he heard something crack. Dean stared at him as Sloane turned the engine on with a harsh twist of the key, forcing his gaze away from his friend.

It took all his willpower not to look in the rearview mirror as he twisted the car out of the parking spot and onto the road. The last thing he needed was to get a final look at Dean's wounded and angry expression. It was bad enough to have seen it for most of that disorienting altercation, and it was worse to see it deepen as Sloane fled.

And all he could think as he drove back to the base was, what the hell had happened?

DEAN

⌘

"Dean, it's okay," Marco's voice assured him over the line.

Dean shoved his phone against his shoulder as he dug through his pocket. "It is *not* okay. As a matter of fact, this is about as far from okay as it gets."

"Okay, well, maybe it's not, but getting mad isn't going to help," Marco said.

"I'm not getting mad. I'm still mad. Fucking asshole," Dean grunted, trying to grab the keys buried at the bottom of his jeans pocket.

"Alright, but have you considered that you were slow to tell him about us for a reason? Maybe you knew this was coming, and maybe it's not all that bad?"

"How is this not bad? He was horrible!"

"He was a little...rude, yeah, you got me there. But c'mon, the two of you have been close for a while now, and he's bound to feel out of sorts after having this dropped in his lap."

Dean hooked his finger through the keyring and yanked the whole collection out with a satisfied grunt. "I didn't drop anything in his lap. For God's sake, Marco, the man is my best friend. He shouldn't be pissed off that I'm dating. It's not like I got mad whenever he was dating someone."

"I thought you said he doesn't date."

"He doesn't, not seriously, but there could have been, at any time, and I didn't act like a complete shit about it."

"No, but you're also not him. You told me he's pretty protective and a little territorial."

Dean frowned. "How does this not bother you?"

"It bothers me because you're so upset."

"Oh God, don't pull the good guy card right now. That just makes me feel even worse."

Marco sighed. "That's the problem. You're taking this like you're somehow responsible for it, and you're not. On some level, you knew there might be a problem, and now you see you were right. Just give him and give you some time to breathe and figure it out. I bet this was just a knee-jerk response on his part. If he's as good a guy as you say he is, he's going to feel like dirt."

"Which he should!"

"Dean."

"Well, he should."

Marco paused. "You're...standing outside his apartment building right now, aren't you?"

"We need to talk," Dean said.

"Or, you could step back and breathe. If you go in there, one or both of you could end up saying something you'll regret."

"I think he has that covered already."

"Well, I'm not going to try and stop you, but I will say that I don't think it's a good idea with you locked in the throes of a pissed-off mood."

"Duly noted."

"But disregarded?"

"Completely."

Marco sighed heavily. "Okay, well, if you need to talk after you're...done, just give me a call, or just summon me over."

Dean grunted. "Thanks."

"Talk to you soon."

Dean ended the call, sliding his phone back into his pocket and twirling the keys around his finger as he stared at the front door to Sloane's apartment building. He knew Sloane was home because he wasn't scheduled for a shift today. Dean had already called the guardhouse and checked. Sloane wasn't known for a whole lot of socializing, and he tended to stay at home on his days off or at Dean's.

Before he could think too hard about how right Marco probably was, Dean stomped toward the door and up the stairs to Sloane's apartment. Swinging the keys one more time, he flipped the key he needed forward and jammed it into the lock. To his surprise, the door opened easily, without him needing to unlock the deadbolt. Despite being on the relative safety of the base, Sloane's childhood growing up in the seedier parts of Chicago had ingrained a lifelong habit of security, and he never kept his deadbolt unlocked.

"Sloane?" Dean called as he stepped through the door, glancing around.

Sloane's wry voice followed a thump from the kitchen. "You're a couple of hours later than I expected."

Dean frowned. "The door was unlocked."

"Yeah, I knew you'd be coming."

Well, that solved that mystery, at least. And with that, Dean's temporary worry faded, and his anger slammed back into place.

"Well, at least you know why I'm here," Dean grunted, shoving the door closed.

Sloane appeared in the doorway, wiping his hands with a

hand towel. "There really aren't that many reasons you'd be here right now."

Dean cocked his head. "Yeah, you're right. Especially when the guy who's supposed to be my best friend, and support me in shit, decides to act like a complete dick for no reason."

Sloane's brow shot up. "Really, we're going to pull the best friend card now?"

"Yeah, Sloane. I am. Because last I checked, that's what best friends were supposed to do, back each other up. What you did last night was the complete opposite."

Sloane chucked the towel somewhere out of sight. "Yeah, and best friends aren't supposed to keep things from one another, but guess what you did?"

Dean motioned to Sloane. "Wow, I wonder why I was so worried about telling you? Maybe it's because of the exact way you acted last night?"

Never had he been so frustrated with Sloane. Dean wasn't so blind he didn't see that Sloane could be excessively grouchy and more than a little aggressive at times. For the most part, Dean was willing to shrug it off, knowing most of it was all bark, and sometimes, he even found it amusing. Typically, Dean could pull Sloane back from the edge if his friend grew too aggressive or mean, and it had *never* been focused on something or someone close to Dean.

Until now.

Sloane crossed his arms. "You've been seeing this guy for weeks, keeping it from me. Then you tell me, and just what? Expect me to be instantly okay with you keeping shit from me?"

"You were the one who said you were perfectly fine with meeting him!" Dean shot back.

"What the fuck else was I supposed to say, Dean? One

I'M STRAIGHT, RIGHT?

minute everything is fine, then I find out you've been seeing someone and doing it for weeks without so much as a mention."

Dean growled. "What the fuck does it matter?"

"It matters because you were keeping it a secret."

"Again, we go right back to you being a giant dick to someone who didn't deserve it! If your issue was with me, you should have said something to me instead of taking it out on Marco for no good fucking reason."

"Maybe I don't like him."

"Maybe you're an asshole."

Sloane's nostrils flared. "We already knew that."

Dean narrowed his eyes, stomping up to Sloane. "Which was fine when you weren't doing it to someone I gave a shit about, and you fucking know it. You knew damn well I was into Marco and that it meant something to me, and you were *still* a giant asshole to him."

Sloane glared, his jaw tightening. "Then maybe you shouldn't have kept him a secret from me."

Dean let out a cry of frustration. "And *maybe* I shouldn't have to report every little detail of my life to you in order to make sure you aren't a bastard to someone."

Sloane dropped his arms, balling his hands into fists at his side. "And why is this any different, hmm?"

Dean hesitated, accusing finger drooping as he felt the weight of Sloane's question fall around him. "What...what?"

"Why is this suddenly different from anything else? Why can you tell me about when your mom found you with your boyfriend before you enlisted? Why can you tell me about how you secretly hate guns? Why can you tell me about, fuck, I don't know, the last time you hooked up, but you can't tell me that you're seeing some guy?"

Dean's chest tightened, and he brought a hand protectively to it. "How do you have the balls to ask me that after last night?"

"Don't change the fucking subject, Dean."

"The entire subject was about you acting like a complete and utter asshole in the first place!"

Sloane's eyes flashed. "And I just fucking told you I'm pissed you decided to keep it a secret from me! So how about you tell me why you thought you needed to keep this a secret when you tell me about anything fucking else."

Dean stepped back, grinding his teeth. "Because you can be a dick."

"I have *never* been an asshole to you before. I have never treated you as anything but the best friend you are. So why the hell would you think it was necessary to keep it from me?"

"Sloane," Dean warned.

"You could have just casually mentioned you were going on a date. Or shit, mentioned you'd had a date and how great it was."

"Sloane."

"You could have told me after the second date. You could have told me after you guys decided to fuck. Hell, you told me any other time you fucked someone, why not this time?"

"Sloane."

Sloane was practically bellowing. "So why not this time, Dean? Huh? Why not this fucking time?"

Dean's temper snapped, and he shoved Sloane away from him. "Because it's been hard enough being in fucking love with you for almost six goddamn years!"

Sloane stumbled, taken off guard by Dean's words and his shove and gaped. "What?"

Dean's eyes stung as he realized what he was saying, but he'd been pushed into a corner and unable to help himself.

The truth was out in that one instant, and the rest poured from him as he forced himself to grip his shirt desperately.

"For six fucking years, I've been hanging on to some stupid, thin thread, swinging back and forth between hoping and knowing it will never happen. I've been crazy about you since we first became friends. Maybe it wasn't that deep initially, but I knew how I felt by the time we left Basic. All I've wanted for six years, six *fucking* years, was you, Sloane."

It felt like his lungs were on fire as he heaved in a gasp of air, trying to keep his voice steady but knowing he was failing. Dean remembered what it had been like alone and trapped behind a dune as armed insurgents bore down on him, pouring bullets into the air around him. Trapped, with limited ammunition and no one close, Dean had faced down the inevitability of his death and, perhaps, even his capture. Staring death in the face had been so much easier than speaking the words that felt as though they were being ripped from his throat, but they kept coming.

"It's taken me this long even to start to get over it, to accept the fact that no matter how great we are together, this is all we'll ever be. And you know what? I've had to accept that this is fine, that this is wonderful. So long as I have a friend like you, I can be okay, even if it's not exactly what I wanted. I worked at it, I fought for it, I fucking lost my shit over it, but I finally got to the point where I could try."

Sloane hadn't moved, his eyes wide as he leaned against the wall silently. Dean took a step away, reeling from the emotions pounding through him. It felt like if he didn't find a way to calm down, his chest would burst.

"And I did it, okay? I got out there, and I found Marco. And he's good to me. He's funny, smart, and good-looking. And every fucking time I'm with him, I have to remind myself that he's *not you*. And he never will be, and I have to be okay with that. So yeah, telling you, the man I've been secretly pining for like some lovesick, stupid thirteen-year-old for six years, would have been too much for me until I had the fucking courage to say it out loud and face the truth that you'll never, *never* love me like I love you."

Dean's voice finally failed him, trailing into a faint whisper, so quiet it wouldn't have been heard if the apartment hadn't been dead silent. Sloane stared at him, the hand held against the wall slowly dropping to his side. Seconds ticked by as they stared at one another, and the reality of what Dean had done began to sink in.

Sloane's voice shook when he finally spoke. "Dean—"

Whatever remained of Dean's courage and willpower snapped, and he turned and fled. Sloane called out after him, and Dean ignored it, shoving through the door and down the stairs. As soon as the outside air hit him, Dean took a huge, wretched gasp as his feet almost tangled around one another, spilling him onto the sidewalk.

Not wanting to stay there for too long, and risk Sloane catching up to him, Dean righted himself and kept running. Honestly, he was sure if anyone saw him, they'd wonder what the hell was wrong. His pace wasn't that of a man trying to exercise in his free time, and he certainly wasn't dressed for it. He was gasping like he'd been running for miles but ignored it until he finally reached one of the beaches outside the base.

The sand managed what his feet hadn't, and Dean tripped as the loose sediment gave way, dumping him face-first on the beach. Dean caught himself, bowing his head as his back heaved with each breath. Sweat coated his skin, sand sticking to it as he pushed himself onto his knees.

"Oh fuck," Dean gasped, realizing what he'd done.

All he'd wanted was to chew Sloane out for being an asshole. Maybe they would fight, have it out right there, maybe even throw a punch or two in the process; he didn't know. He'd expected the two of them to face the problem head-on and find a way to get over it just as quickly. Never in his wildest imaginings had he seen himself spilling his secret.

"Oh, fuck. What am I going to do?" he moaned.

SLOANE

Cursing at his phone for being too slow and fickle, he tossed the device onto the desk. It clattered loudly in the silence of the guardhouse, and Sloane heaved himself back in his seat with a grunt. He didn't care if the thing broke; he needed a new one anyway.

"And here I thought being close to the end of your shift would put you in a better mood," Trisha said from her usual spot in the corner.

"You thought wrong," Sloane told her.

"So, any reason you've been a grumpier shit than usual? Or are you just turning your charm up high?"

"I'm not grumpy," Sloane growled.

"Yeah, that was convincing."

Sloane pressed his lips together, refusing to take the bait. Trisha clicked her tongue but said nothing else as she returned her attention to her book. She at least could be trusted to leave him alone when he clearly didn't want to be bothered. Simmons had nearly driven Sloane to commit murder the day before, and Sloane was glad he was able to get through a shift without the man around.

I'M STRAIGHT, RIGHT?

Annoyed, he snatched up his phone to recheck it despite no buzz or flashing light to signify a notification. Unsurprisingly, the screen was empty of messages, and he let out another low growl. It had been over four days since he and Dean's blowout and since Dean had fled Sloane's apartment. Four days of not a single word or appearance on Dean's part, and Sloane didn't know what to do. They had never had a huge fight before, and Sloane didn't know what to do with a Dean who was both hurt and furious with him.

And then there was what Dean had said.

Trisha cleared her throat, jerking him out of his thoughts. His eyes snapped toward her, and the woman nodded toward the clock. It had slipped toward the end of his shift, with some time to spare, and he hadn't noticed. Trisha wasn't normally one to push him out the door, and Sloane took that as an indicator of how cranky he had been. It didn't change his mood in the slightest. If anything, it added more surliness on top.

"See you tomorrow," she said as he heaved himself out of his chair.

Not before he worked a few hours with Simmons first, a prospect he wasn't looking forward to. The guy normally irritated him no more than most people, but lately, he'd grown even more aggravating. It had taken all Sloane's willpower to stay relatively calm, reminding himself it wasn't Simmons' fault that he was in such a foul mood.

The mood seemed to emanate from him more than usual if the people he passed on the way back to his apartment were any indication. A few people who were friendly with him raised their hands in greeting, only for their arms to drop to their side as they averted their eyes. Sloane didn't think he looked *that* grumpy, but the continued avoidance of other people was both welcome and irritating.

Sloane had just slammed his apartment door closed when

his phone started buzzing. Fumbling to pull the device out, he nearly dropped it in his haste. A flash of disappointment, followed by guilt, shot through him as he took in the picture of his mother on the caller ID. Sighing, he flopped onto the edge of a nearby seat, answering the phone and pressing it to his face before bending over to unlace his boots.

"What's up?" Sloane asked.

His mother's wry tone answered. "Oh, you sound like you're in a lovely mood."

"I always sound in a bad mood, something everyone likes to remind me of."

"I don't think you sound like that."

"Except for right now."

His mother chuckled. "I'm not the only one. Shawna told me you were 'meaner than usual' to her."

Sloane kicked a boot off with a snort. "I wasn't mean to her. I told her the truth."

"With all the grace and tact we expect from you, I'm sure."

"If she wanted that, she should've asked you for advice. I can't help it if she repeatedly runs into the same problems with these boys. You're living with her; you should know what she's up to."

"I also remember someone having a problem with a handful of girls at that age."

"I didn't go crying to everyone else about it."

There was a pause before his mother spoke again, worry in her voice. "I don't want to pry too much, Sloane, but this doesn't sound like you. I know your sister tries your patience, but you've never spoken about her like this before."

Sloane sighed heavily. "I know, I'm sorry. I know she's not 'crying' about anything. I'm just being an ass."

"Normally, that would have me making a joke, but this doesn't sound like your normal bluntness."

Sloane stood up, shifting the phone around as he yanked his top off. "I'm just...grumpy."

His mother clicked her tongue. "Really?"

"Yes, really."

"Sloane."

He *hated* it when she took that tone with him. There were very few people in the world capable of making him feel like he was being a stubborn ass just because he was keeping things to himself. Even fewer people could get away with it, including his mother and Dean.

"Mom," Sloane warned, grinding his teeth.

"Do not make me invoke the full name."

Sloane cringed. "Mama."

"Don't you 'Mama' me. You tell me what's got you in such a foul mood."

"It's nothing, Mama," Sloane protested.

"You got to the count of five."

Sloane tightened his grip. "I don't negotiate with terrorists."

"One."

"Mom, seriously."

"Two."

"I'm not ten years old anymore!"

"Three."

"It won't work."

"*Four.*"

"Mama..."

"Fi—"

"Dean and I had a fight!" Sloane finally snapped.

There was another pause, followed by a sigh. "Well, that explains why you're not talking about this with him, at least."

Sloane slumped onto his couch. "You don't sound surprised."

"Honey, you two have been friends since you met, what, six years ago?"

"Sounds right."

"It's honestly a surprise you haven't fought until now."

Sloane frowned. "Thanks, Mom."

She huffed. "You listen to me. I'm not saying that as anything against either of you, but let's be honest, people fight. It's what they do. Personalities clash, people get ideas stuck in their heads and let them fester, and sometimes, we say the wrong thing at the wrong time. Any of those things and more can make even the best of friends turn on one another and have it out. It's a sign of how well you get along that it hasn't happened till now, but it was bound to happen."

"Especially when you think about how pleasant I am," Sloane huffed.

"Hard to love isn't the same as not worth being loved, and you are."

"You're my mom. You're supposed to say that shit."

"Dean obviously thinks so, too."

Sloane closed his eyes, forcing himself to take a deep breath. Apparently, Dean thought Sloane was worth loving in a way he'd never expected. Dean's words echoed in his head, and Sloane felt another headache coming on.

"Yeah, I guess."

"There's no guessing about it. He loves you, just like we do. Now, you want to tell me what the fight was about?"

Sloane groaned. "Not really."

"Because you think it's ridiculous or because of you?"

Sloane frowned. "Why do you have to think I'm responsible?"

"Please, I raised you, remember? If this were his fault or something that just happened, you'd tell me. If you're a big reason it happened, you're going to shut your mouth and keep it to yourself. You did it when you broke the microwave."

"I was eight!"

"And some things never change."

Sloane's shoulders dropped. "I...freaked a little."

"How much is a little?"

"Dean's been seeing someone."

"Okay, where's the problem?"

"He's been seeing someone, and I think it's been for weeks, and I only found out because I happened to stumble across them while they were out on a date."

She made a soft noise. "I see, so he didn't tell you."

"No."

"And you took it badly."

"I might have been...a little rude. Okay, I was really rude, and it felt like I was beating up the poor bastard who didn't do shit wrong except like my best friend. And Dean kept looking like I kicked his puppy."

"Doesn't sound like the Dean you've talked about."

Sloane grunted. "Yeah, he saved that for later when he caught me alone."

"And gave you an earful."

"And then some."

Sloane had thought he was prepared for the showdown with Dean. He had, after all, been out of line and reacted poorly to a situation that Sloane knew was out of character for Dean. That Dean had hidden something so...normal from Sloane should have been a warning sign there was more at play. Instead, Sloane had let his stung feelings and wounded pride get the better of him, and the next thing he knew, he was emotionally shoving Dean into a corner.

"Alright, so you fought because he kept something from you."

"I was just...so mad, Mama. Why would he keep that from

me? Why wouldn't he tell me? I kept thinking maybe he thought I might be upset because, suddenly, the whole gay thing would be real to me. Or that I might be a dick to someone new because everyone expects it from me," Sloane admitted.

"And then you turned around and did just that."

Sloane rubbed a hand over his face vigorously. "I know I was an ass, okay? I know that, and I was an even bigger ass when he was here, trying to tell me off for being an ass. I thought I would apologize and maybe try to figure out what was wrong with him. Then he was here, and I just got so mad, I was pissed. I kept demanding he tell me why, why he did it, why he would keep it from me, just why, why, why. And then—"

"And then?"

Sloane shook his head. "Then, I found out why."

"Honey, Sloane, talk to me. You know nothing you say leaves this phone."

Sloane knew, but that didn't make it any easier to say. Dean's secret had come out in such a desperate, raw moment of pure emotion. Sloane had never seen such pure agony on Dean's face, and the sound of his friend's heart breaking in front of him had left Sloane dumbfounded. It had taken him several minutes before his brain had clicked into place, realizing he should have tried to stop Dean from leaving before it was too late.

"He's been in love with me, Mama," Sloane heard himself say.

"Oh."

A sad smile crossed Sloane's face, and he nodded in the face of his mother's breathless understanding. No doubt she wondered the same things Sloane had since Dean had dropped the news. How many times had Dean taken a hug from Sloane as a sign of something more? How often had

Sloane unthinkingly paraded himself on display, teasing Dean? They had been friends for years, and Sloane had unthinkingly tormented his best friend with hopes of something else between them, and a piece of Sloane died every time he realized.

And he couldn't help but wonder what Dean saw in that thread of possibility.

His mother cleared her throat. "That would explain why he was so slow to tell you about this new guy."

"It does?" Sloane asked with an incredulous laugh.

"Because of his feelings for you."

"Again, that makes sense?"

"In his heart, he's still got feelings for you, Sloane. Feelings he never planned on telling you. Despite that, I think he took a big risk, privately, by seeing this new guy. I think, deep down, he felt that by committing to this new guy, he would finally have to leave what he felt he could have with you behind."

Sloane frowned. "That doesn't make sense."

She laughed. "And when have people ever made sense? The heart wants what it wants, and we're stuck riding out the waves it creates. He's been living life knowing he has to let go of you, in that way, but afraid to do so." She hesitated. "Though I can see what he saw."

Sloane pulled the phone away from his ear to give it a bewildered look before replacing it. "Excuse me?"

"I just mean, the two of you are a good pair. You mesh well. Dean accepts you the way you are but doesn't let you get away with murder. You keep him out of his head too much, but you make sure he's still himself. There's an ebb and flow to the way you both work. In all honesty, if you were even remotely interested in men, I'd be telling you you're an idiot for not snatching him up while you have the chance."

Sloane sat, letting her words sink in slowly. While it hurt his heart to remember the times he'd made a passing comment about how good he and Dean would be if he were into guys, he realized he had accidentally stumbled upon the truth in those moments. Having Dean around was soothing, comforting, a balm to Sloane's frazzled nerves. And Dean always seemed so much happier, so much more himself around Sloane. It was as though the two of them brought something to the table the other needed without any effort whatsoever.

They just worked.

"I'm not that person," Sloane finally said, his stomach growing more leaden.

"I'm only saying it's a pity you're not."

Sloane couldn't find any argument with that.

"How do I fix this, Mama?"

"I'm sorry, Sloane, but you can't fix his heart. You can't give him what his heart desires, and he's going to hurt over that. It's inevitable."

His heart sank, and he nodded, knowing it was the truth before she'd even said it but hating it all the same. Sloane already felt helpless in the face of whatever demons Dean had dragged back from the desert, and now this?

"How can I help him without making things worse?" Sloane asked softly.

"Be there for him, Sloane. When he's ready to come around, when he's ready to move forward, be there for him. You can't fix this, but the worst thing you can do is hide from him or pull away. Right now, he's revealed his darkest secret to you, and he needs time to make peace with that. When he does, you need to be what you've always been, his best friend."

Was that possible after what Dean had told him? Sloane would gladly give Dean whatever he wanted, whatever he needed, but would Dean be able to look him in the eye again? Would the two of them ever be able to get back to what they had been, or had things between them changed forever?

Sloane's gut twisted, and some part of him believed it was the latter.

"I just...want him back," Sloane admitted.

"Then be there when he comes back, and he'll stay."

DEAN

Dean shoved his way through the double doors to the clinic, barely noticing as one of them bounced off the wall with a bang. At the end of the hallway, Troy stood, spinning around at the loud noise and staring at Dean.

"Uh, morning?" Troy asked.

"Morning," Dean replied tersely.

It was then he spotted someone else with Troy and hesitated. Private John Simmons was standing in the doorway of one of the exam rooms, staring at Dean.

Dean raised a brow. "What?"

Simmons blinked. "Uh, nothing?"

Dean looked at Troy. "He have an appointment?"

Troy smiled. "People can come in here without an appointment, Dean, that's...kind of how this works."

Dean rolled his eyes. "Save your jokes for the patients, Troy. Excuse me."

He pushed his way past the two men and into his small cubicle. Plopping down, he jammed his finger on the power button of his computer, cursing when he realized it had already been on. Fuming, he waited until it finished its shut-down procedure so he could turn it back on again.

"Shit, what's wrong with Doc?" he heard Simmons mutter.

"Um, he's been like that for about a week now just...don't mind him."

"Fuck, man, Sloane almost took my head off today when I asked him what time he got off his shift. Think that's got anything to do with it?"

Dean shoved at his desk, rolling over to the doorway with a clatter. "I think the two of you should stop gossiping and get back to what you're here for in the first place. How about that?"

Troy turned, giving Simmons a shove toward the room. "Right, get your ass in there before you get us both killed."

"Man, no one likes questions around here," Simmons grumbled as he was pushed away.

Dean continued to glower until the two men were out of sight. That accomplished, he pushed back toward the computer just in time for it to pop up with the login screen. Ignoring the faint sound of quiet voices down the hall, he tapped at the keyboard, jabbing the enter button to get his day started.

The sound of soft footsteps coming up the hallway sent his heart racing. Few people walked that quietly, especially without their presence being announced by the sound of the door. Dean looked up to the doorway of his cubicle, wondering if he wanted it to be Sloane or terrified that it would be. He was spared by the presence of Marco, his hazel eyes shifting over Dean's face before smiling gently.

Shoving his faint disappointment aside, Dean returned the smile. "Hey, Marco."

"I can tell you're not feeling much better."

Dean sighed. "No, not really."

Marco leaned against the doorway. "Want to talk about it?"

"No, but I'm open to drinking about it."

"Is this the part where I remind you you already did that?"

Dean winced. "Can we not?"

The last thing he needed was to remember how abysmally drunk he'd gotten while he was supposed to be on a date with Marco earlier that week. As far as he knew, he hadn't made a complete idiot of himself, but just the knowledge that he'd been drunk off his ass was enough to make him cringe. His attempts at making light of the situation bit him in the ass as surely as losing his temper with Sloane had.

"I know things have been a little...tense for you," Marco began.

Dean snorted. "That's one way to describe it."

"Which is why I called. You were all but mute yesterday."

Dean blinked, staring at the blank spot on the wall as he analyzed what Marco had said. After a moment, he realized the man was absolutely right. Dean had been so caught up in what he'd been doing he hadn't touched his phone more than a few times throughout the day. True, the clinic had been busier than usual, a distraction Dean had welcomed, but Dean hadn't been any better by the time he got back to his apartment.

Dean winced. "I'm sorry. I guess I'm more out of it than I thought."

"You're fine. Last I checked, Sloane was not only your best friend but someone you've never fought with before. This has got to be weird for you both."

Dean laughed. "How are you still willing to give him credit? He didn't exactly make a good first impression."

"Anyone you're willing to devote this much emotional energy to must be worth it. I can't see you being this close to someone who was awful. He might have been...abrasive when I met him, but considering the circumstances, I can't say I blame him."

Dean couldn't even summon the energy to be mad at Sloane for that anymore. His friend had been taken so off-guard, no mean feat considering Sloane was pretty steady, and the realization that Dean had been keeping something from him had stung. Sloane might not want to admit it, but Dean knew his friend, and the man would have taken Dean keeping secrets as not just an insult, but he would have felt snubbed.

And looking back on it, Dean couldn't blame him.

Dean looked up again, shaking his head. "What are you doing here?"

Marco chuckled, walking forward to sit on the edge of Dean's desk. "Well, like I said, after you were quiet yesterday, I grew concerned. You've been trying to look like you're okay, but you're obviously not."

It didn't help that Dean hadn't told Marco what had driven Dean from Sloane's apartment. Just as Dean had found it too hard to tell Sloane about Marco, he point-blank refused to tell Marco about his feelings for Sloane, especially because they were still present, even though he was trying his hardest to move past them.

When did he become hellbent on holding on to so many secrets from those he cared about?

Marco took Dean's hand gently in his, squeezing it. "Have you thought about talking to him?"

Dean looked down at his phone. "I've tried to text him a dozen times and deleted them halfway. I dial his number and immediately hang up."

"Here's a thought. Have you tried just simply finding Sloane and talking to him face to face?"

Dean had, but the idea made his already upset stomach do flips non-stop. What exactly was he supposed to say to

Sloane? Dean had dumped the reality of his true feelings in the man's lap without even the benefit of tact as a buffer. Everything Dean had felt, anguished over and held tight within himself, had spilled forth. Dean knew the phrase about dams bursting, but never had he felt such a torrent of emotions pour from him before, and he still didn't know what to think about it.

Sloane couldn't have been in a better place over it, either. The shock on Sloane's face was burned into Dean's memory. His friend had never known, never suspected, and it had struck him like a sucker punch. How exactly was Dean supposed to face him after that?

"Considered it, but then I also considered finding a big rock and living under it for the rest of my life."

Marco's mouth twitched. "My little hermit crab."

Dean smiled but couldn't think what to add to the endearment that wasn't depressing. He thought he'd spent enough time scuttling through the sand to last a lifetime. Images of towering mountains of sand, interspersed with sunbaked stretches of dirt, rose in his mind. Dean took a deep breath, focusing on the sharp smell of antiseptic and the rich scent of food sitting in front of him before his mind went from desolate sands to blood and screaming.

"Dean?" Marco asked worriedly.

Dean gave him a light squeeze, smiling. "Just thinking a little too hard, sorry."

He wasn't Marco's, any more than the other man was his. The night Sloane had stumbled across them, Dean had finally been trying to find the courage to make whatever he and Marco had more official. It would have been nice to say he had a boyfriend, but the sudden presence and fallout of his best friend finding them had shot that in the face. Now, he couldn't summon the energy to take that last step with Marco.

Dean closed his eyes, promising that when he'd settled things with Sloane, he would ask Marco to be his boyfriend.

"Look," Marco began.

Dean's eyes snapped open, eyeing him warily. "Please tell me you're not about to tell me we should just be friends."

Marco hesitated for the briefest of moments before shaking his head. "That's not what I was going to say."

Dean narrowed his eyes. "I don't think I can handle anything else being thrown at me right now...shit, wait, that's not fair to you, is it?"

Marco hopped off the desk and knelt before Dean. "Hey, it's okay. I'm not ending things or walking away, alright? Unless you choose to walk away, or there's a very good reason for me...to step aside, I'm not going to, alright."

Dean tilted his head, slowly nodding. "Okay."

"I was going to say that maybe you should talk to Sloane. I bet he's just as miserable as you are right now."

Dean thought about what he'd heard Simmons muttering to Troy and sighed. It wasn't exactly a surprise to hear that Sloane was more surly than usual. Sloane had always been a little bad-tempered, but if he was grumpy enough that someone who worked with him regularly commented on it, Sloane must have been spitting nails.

"And what if he's still mad?" Dean asked, fearing it might be even worse than just mad.

"I don't think he was mad in the first place. Do you?"

"No, God, it sounds so childish, but I think I hurt his feelings."

Marco winked. "You're never too old to get your feelings hurt, Dean. And before you get that guilty look on your face, sometimes you hurt someone's feelings without meaning to. No one's perfect, and let's be honest, it's true what they say. We always hurt the ones we love the most."

Dean frowned. "That's not really supposed to make me feel better, is it?"

"Give it a little thought, and maybe it will make you feel better. You've got to forgive yourself for being human. We're all flawed."

"You sound more like a therapist than a tech guy," Dean observed.

Marco leaned back, mock preening. "Well, as your senior, I have some life experience under my belt. I've accumulated a bit of wisdom in my time."

Dean snorted, swatting Marco's chest gently. "You're a whole three years older, don't start."

Marco caught his hand, standing up. "I mean it, though. Stop punishing yourself for this and go talk to him. If you ask me, you're both going to be really awkward. Try to talk about it, and realize you simply want your friendship back. You'll do it, and things will get back to normal, and when they are, you can deal with the problem at hand."

"You make it sound a lot easier than it feels."

Something unreadable flicked across Marco's eyes and was gone before Dean could register what it was.

"You two are incredibly close, and that sort of bond doesn't get thrown away over one fight."

Dean chewed his lip, unsure, considering the parts Marco didn't know.

Marco squeezed his hand again. "Just give it some thought. Can you promise me that?"

Dean huffed, shaking his head. "Yeah, I can do that."

"Without drinking?"

Dean looked up, narrowing his eyes. "Without drinking."

Marco bent forward, kissing his cheek gently. "Good, you'll be doing yourself and your liver a favor."

Dean smiled, watching him go even as his mind ran over everything they'd discussed. He desperately wanted Marco to be right and for him and Sloane to ultimately find a way to get beyond what had happened. Dean wanted to believe his and Sloane's friendship was strong enough to move past even Dean's surprise revelation and that he wasn't going to lose the best friendship he'd ever known and one of the greatest people he'd ever known.

Hope flickered in Dean's chest, even as he wondered why it felt as though Marco was slipping away.

SLOANE

Stumbling through his door, Sloane cursed as the bottle tucked into the crook of his arm almost dislodged itself. Fumbling, he wiggled his arm up and caught it before it shattered on the floor. Struggling with the plastic bags in hand, he made his way past the living room and into the kitchen.

Sloane dropped the bags, grumbling as he grabbed the liquor and set it on the counter, where it would no longer be in danger. As he bent down to grab the bags to unload them, he froze, his mind finally catching up with what his eyes had seen as he came through the door.

Backing up, Sloane stepped into the dining room and leaned back so he could see into his living room. Sat in the big plush chair against the far wall, staring intently at him, was a nervous-looking Dean.

"Hey," Dean said.

Sloane blinked. "Hey."

He wanted to feel relief that Dean was there, but Sloane was still trying to process the reality of Dean's presence. Normally, there was a sign, shoes kicked off, and in the way, a jacket haphazardly thrown over the chair, an empty water bottle left on a table, anything to mark Dean's presence. Yet Sloane had walked right past him, spotting him but not registering that he was there.

"Sorry to drop in like this. I wanted to call first, but I'm kind of shit at making phone calls, so I just made myself come here and wait instead," Dean said, his hands clasped in front of him.

"You're always welcome here, Dean," Sloane said, stepping into the living room.

Dean looked up, searching Sloane's face. "I know, but after...well—"

Sloane nodded, noticing the dark circles under Dean's eyes and the stubble on his face. Dean wasn't the most organized or neat person when he was off the clock, but he took care of his appearance. He certainly didn't look a mess, but Sloane could see he was off-kilter.

"Not been sleeping?" Sloane asked.

Dean looked as though he might deny it and then shrugged. "Dreams."

"*The* dreams?" Sloane asked.

Dean gave another shrug. "And other ones."

Once again, Sloane wanted to ask what was in those dreams and what had caused them. However, he knew it wasn't the right time, especially since Dean looked so vulnerable. The last thing Sloane wanted was to push Dean into another corner, forcing an emotional outburst Dean wasn't ready for.

Again.

Sloane had never been very good at expressing himself, not with words anyway. Whenever he tried, he stumbled over his words, sometimes making the situation even worse. He'd never had that trouble with Dean, though. No matter what, Sloane had always known what to say or do when it came to Dean. To feel at an utter loss the way he did now, looking into Dean's wary, aching expression, was new and awful.

Dean cleared his throat. "Look, I know...a lot of things were said the last time I was here. And if I could take it back, I would."

Did Sloane want him to, though? Sloane wished Dean hadn't kept everything to himself, hadn't kept his hurt locked away where Sloane would never be able to help even the slightest. Wasn't it better that Sloane knew now, even if the knowledge sat strangely in Sloane's head? It was so odd to think about it. Dean had wanted him. Dean had been in love with him.

Strange and a little intriguing.

"Dean," Sloane began, not quite sure what he was going to say.

Dean shook his head. "Sloane, I'm sorry I dumped that on you, and I'm sorry I freaked out."

"You had every right. I shouldn't have pushed you and…" Sloane stopped, again at a loss.

Dean looked up, making a brave attempt at a smile. "See? I'm not sure what to do about this either. I want it to be better, but I don't know how."

They'd never had to deal with this sort of thing before. Dean was no doubt aching over having spilled his secret the way he had, but Sloane could see it was more than that. Neither of them had fought with the other. Sure, there had been bickering, and they weren't afraid to give each other hell, but they'd never outright fought.

But he couldn't stand to see the pain on Dean's face anymore and decided to go with the truth.

"I want my friend back," Sloane said.

Dean looked up, nervous but nodding. "That's what I want too."

Sloane snorted softly. "Then be my friend again, Dean. If

you've got the time, you could hang out here. We can bullshit, watch shitty movies, and eat junk food. Hell, I just got a fifth of some pretty good vodka. We don't have to talk about this shit, not until we're ready. But until then, let's...just be friends again."

He wouldn't have blamed Dean if the man had insisted on talking things out and settling things right away. But Sloane wasn't surprised to see relief spread over Dean's face, and his shoulders lost some of their tension. Dean had been prepared for anything Sloane was ready to throw at him, but he was also more than happy to take Sloane's offer.

Dean looked up, smiling a little. "Vodka?"

"What? I like vodka."

"You like beer and whiskey. I'm the one who likes vodka."

Sloane shrugged. "Maybe I also bought a few things to go with it."

Dean looked over at Sloane. "Did you buy stuff for my poor man's peach martinis?"

Sloane sighed. "It sounded good, okay?"

"God, I've turned you onto fruity drinks? I never thought I'd see the day."

"Don't start. I'm allowed to enjoy a bit of fruit in my drinks," Sloane growled.

Dean held up his hands in mock surrender. "I'm just saying. You swore up and down you'd never understand why I liked the damn things."

"Until you cheated and gave me those things."

Damn him. Dean knew how much Sloane obsessed over peach flavor.

Dean grinned. "And now you've been converted."

"You want some or not?" Sloane asked with a snort.

"Fine, but I'm not doing it on an empty stomach. Since you got the booze, I'll order some food, burgers?"

"Of fucking course."

Dean grinned, pulling out his phone. "Then burgers it is."

Sloane hesitated at the door. "I'm not getting any say in the movie, though, am I?"

Dean chuckled. "Not a chance."

Sloane let out a pitiful sigh but walked away as though accepting his fate. He stopped in the doorway to the kitchen, glancing back one more time as Dean waited for the burger place to pick up. After days of not having him around, it was a relief beyond anything Sloane had known to see Dean standing in his living room again.

He just wished Dean didn't look so miserable when he thought Sloane wasn't looking.

* * *

"I seriously get to pick the movie next time," Sloane complained.

Dean snickered from his cocoon of blankets. "Hell no, this movie is great."

"I can't tell if this movie is about vampires or if it's supposed to be sci-fi. What I do know is the acting is terrible."

"The fight scenes, though."

"Cheesy and over the top."

"They're amazing, right?"

Sloane knew he wasn't going to win. When it came to horrible action movies, Dean would never be dissuaded. His love of horror movies, gritty thrillers, and dark musicals was an odd combination. Sloane was perfectly content to curl up and watch anything, a product of years of dealing with whatever his mother or sisters threw on the screen. But if he were given a choice, he would have happily settled in with a nice crime drama or, hell, maybe even a cute animal film.

Dean took another drink, humming happily. "I've seen this movie so many times, and I still love it."

Sloane's eyes widened. "You've seen it?"

"Well, yeah. I've pretty much gone through every action movie with a badass bitch in existence."

Sloane eyed the drink in Dean's hand. "Badass bitch, huh? How many have you had?"

"As many as you've had," Dean said, his half-lidded eyes triumphant.

If it was anyone else, Sloane might have had a smart comment, but not with Dean. Although Dean couldn't exactly keep up with Sloane when it came to drinking, he could put away a great deal of alcohol before he became well and truly drunk. Then again, if Sloane was feeling the alcohol buzzing away heavily in his head, he knew Dean had to be even more gone.

"Did we finish it off yet?" Sloane asked, looking down at his empty glass.

"We did, but there's beer," Dean proclaimed happily, tipping the glass from side to side with each syllable.

Sloane chuckled. "Yeah, you're drunk."

Dean beamed, downing the rest of his drink. "And happy to be."

Sloane wasn't going to complain. The shadow that had hung around Dean's face was long gone, replaced by a pleasant glow. The alcohol had definitely helped, as Dean was always a happy drunk. The night had been perfect. Neither of them had addressed the elephant in the room, content to ignore it while they spent time together as they always did.

Sloane pushed himself up, one hand coming out as he felt the room tilt slightly. Chuckling, he made his way into the kitchen, humming as he opened the fridge and dug out a beer. He contemplated grabbing one for Dean, but if Sloane was wobbling as he walked, he suspected Dean didn't need anymore. The thing was, if Dean had a drink in his hand, the man would keep drinking, but if he got drunk enough, he would forget about drinking so long as he wasn't given any. Maybe it was a bit of trickery, but Sloane thought it was the good kind that kept Dean from ending up with one hell of a hangover the next day.

When he entered the living room, Dean had flopped on his side, spread out along the couch. Sloane snorted, stopping at the end where he'd been sitting, now occupied by Dean's head.

"Really?" Sloane asked.

Dean looked up, wide-eyed. "I'm comfy."

Sloane rolled his eyes. "Lift your head, you lazy shit."

Dean did as he was told, and Sloane returned to his spot. Sloane watched as Dean laid his head on Sloane's thigh, placing his hand above Sloane's knee as he made himself comfortable. He thought it was telling that Dean didn't hesitate in the slightest at cuddling up close despite having told Sloane his secret.

The thought rippled through him, and Sloane took a deep drink of his beer. He wondered just how much Dean had struggled at moments like this when he was curled up against Sloane, comfortable and affectionate. Had Dean not given too much thought to his feelings in those moments, somehow separating what he felt from the happiness? Or had he struggled the whole way through, wishing it was something more while knowing he would get nothing else?

Sloane frowned, struggling to make sense of the idea that Dean had been suffering the entire time they'd been friends. Would Sloane have been able to do the same? While he certainly respected boundaries and wasn't exactly loose, he'd never been one to deny himself. If there was someone he wanted, Sloane wasn't shy about pursuing them, perfectly willing to accept the possibility of being shot down.

Would he have been able to do the same if he were in Dean's shoes?

"You have to admire the choreography," Dean said, eyes riveted on the screen.

Sloane snorted. "I admire the fact that you can say choreography without slurring like an idiot."

Dean's fingers squeezed his leg as he laughed. "Ass."

A jolt shot through him at the pressure on his leg, and whatever Sloane might have shot back was lost in his shock. Glad Dean wasn't paying attention, Sloane gazed down at his friend in wonder. They'd done this several times, with Dean curled and comfy, holding onto Sloane. He'd never given it any thought before, taking it for what it was.

Sloane reached down, hesitating for a moment before finally resting his hand on Dean's head. That, too, was normal, with Sloane's fingers rubbing against Dean's head and down over his neck gently. Little touches, gestures, ones they had done a million times before, except now Sloane knew what had been locked away in Dean's head.

Had there been more than just struggle, disappointment, and bitter hope for Dean in their affectionate moments? Had he also laid his head upon Sloane's lap and known he was mere inches away from Sloane's cock? Sloane had never given too much thought to the sexual side of Dean's life, but surely he had to have had thoughts, desires. If Sloane were in his place, he would have thought of it easily, especially when their bodies were so close and access to his fantasies was within reach.

Dean closed his eyes as Sloane's fingers reached his neck, digging into the muscles with practiced ease. At the same time, Dean's fingers stroked Sloane's thigh, a low, happy noise rumbling out of him.

"You okay?" Sloane asked, bewildered as his heart pounded.

Dean slid his head further up Sloane's thigh, nodding. "It feels really good. Maybe you could be a masseur if you ever get out."

Had Dean ever been turned on by Sloane's touches?

The thought wouldn't leave Sloane, bringing a surge of unbidden images to mind as he gazed back on all the times they'd sat like this. Dean pressed against his lap, fingers lying casually upon Sloane's body, but in his mind, Dean's head turned toward Sloane's crotch, careful fingers finding their way to his zipper and button, slowly undoing them as he reached into Sloane's pants. Sloane closed his eyes, shaking his head as images of Dean's mouth closing around him came next.

Pressure against his thigh brought his eyes open. Dean had turned around, using one hand against Sloane's leg to prop himself up. His dark eyes swam with worry as he looked at him.

"You okay?" Dean asked.

Sloane cleared his throat. "I don't know."

He didn't; he really didn't. Never had he dared to think of Dean in a sexual sense, and now he was staring at Dean's lips and wondering. Was it because of Dean's confession, digging its way into Sloane's skull and leaving him to wonder in an attempt to understand Dean's perspective? If that were true, why was his heart beating so hard, and why were the thoughts so damned intrusive?

Dean frowned, his mouth opening and then freezing in place. For a moment, Sloane wasn't sure what was wrong until Dean's fingers twitched against his cock. As one, both of them looked down to where Dean's hand pressed against Sloane's leg and stared. Without realizing it, Sloane had grown rock hard right along the inside seam of his pants until it had pressed against Dean's fingers.

Dean looked up, eyes wide. "Sloane?"

He was hard because of his thoughts about Dean, because of Dean himself.

"Oh," Sloane whispered.

Time stood still as Dean gazed at him, and Sloane gazed back. Neither moved as Sloane's cock pressed insistently against the fabric of his jeans, and Dean never moved his grip. Sloane knew he needed to say something, explain it, make it easier, anything at all, but he could barely keep his breathing in check.

Then Dean's hand moved, fingers closing around the impression of Sloane's cock, and what left his mouth was a low moan. Dean's dark eyes grew almost black as his pupils swelled in response to the sound, licking his bottom lip. Sloane stayed still as Dean's fingers traced their way up the length of his cock, stroking back and forth in slow, exploratory motions.

"Sloane?" Dean asked, voice breathless.

He wasn't even going to attempt talking, licking his lips and nodding instead. It was all he could manage, but it seemed enough for Dean, whose hand slid to the button of Sloane's jeans. Watching closely, Sloane's breath stuttered as Dean undid the button, gripping the zipper and sliding it down. Dean's eyes never left his face as he reached in, hesitating when his fingers found bare skin instead of fabric beneath Sloane's jeans.

"Commando again," Dean said.

Sloane huffed. "Again?"

"Think I never noticed that you do it a lot?"

And there it was, confirmation that Dean's attention to Sloane hadn't been totally pure. The realization should have been startling, uncomfortable even, but Sloane's cock gave a twitch instead. Dean's fingers stroked the base of Sloane's cock, and Sloane slid a little lower on the couch, trying to give the man better access.

Dean pushed away from the couch, moving steadily as he crouched, and knelt between Sloane's legs. Sloane's heart thudded so hard, he was shocked they couldn't hear it as Dean took hold of his jeans and pulled them down to his thighs. Sloane's head swam as he watched his best friend kneeling before him, taking hold of the base of his cock to pull it to freedom.

Dean's eyes were locked on Sloane's cock as his fingers ran over the entire thick length, and Sloane wondered if he was going to lose it right there. He froze as Dean leaned forward, wrapping his lips around the head. Warmth spread over his cock, and Sloane let out a low whimper as he felt it slide down further.

Sloane didn't know what was more erotic, the sensation of Dean's mouth around his cock, or the sight of his best friend inching his mouth further down. If he'd been a little more clearheaded, Sloane would have been impressed by just how much of his cock Dean was able to take. Instead, a low moan broke from his lips, and his hand curled behind Dean's head as the muscles of the man's throat gripped him tight.

Pulling back, Dean nursed gently on the head, pulling another low, desperate noise from Sloane. When Dean pushed forward, moaning deeply, Sloane's back arched as pleasure zinged through him like a bolt. It seemed to be all Dean needed, however, and he began to bob in earnest, sucking Sloane into the back of his throat deeper each time.

Sloane sucked in a breath, letting it hiss out between his teeth as Dean's lips, tongue, and throat worked him over. He didn't know if anyone had ever sucked him like this, a mixture of desperate and reverent. Dean's hands gripped Sloane's exposed legs, squeezing the thick muscles as he drove himself forward, embedding Sloane's cock in his throat and holding it there.

Squirming, Sloane pushed his hips up, trying to keep the grip, the warmth, of Dean's mouth around his cock. The muscles of his body curled up, building in pressure and pleasure as Dean allowed him to thrust up into his throat, moaning as Sloane did so. Before completely losing his mind, Sloane willed himself back, panting as he hung at the edge.

"Dean," Sloane groaned, not wanting to force him.

Once more, Dean never hesitated to drive his mouth forward, taking Sloane entirely again. Sloane gave a low cry, fingers tightening into a fist in Dean's hair as he came hard. Around his cock, Dean's mouth and throat vibrated with a groan as Sloane's cock swelled and poured forth. Sloane watched, unable to do anything else, as his orgasm cascaded through him. Dean pulled his head back, holding only the head of Sloane's cock in his mouth and letting him spurt over his tongue.

Sloane was left panting for breath, and Dean eased his mouth gently from Sloane's cock. Dean didn't move from between Sloane's legs, gazing up at him with a blank expression. When his head cleared a little, Sloane gazed back at his friend, his mind a racing, incomprehensible storm.

What had they just done?

DEAN

The first thing he became aware of was how bright the room was. Dean groaned, turning away from the light streaming through the curtains directly across his face. One of these days, he would learn to lay his head on the other side of the couch so he didn't wake up in pain from the brilliance of the cursed fiery orb in the sky.

As much as he would have happily rolled over and gone to sleep again, his bladder began screaming at him. Grunting unhappily, Dean pushed himself up from the couch cushions. However, his movement was a little too sharp, and he almost sent himself tumbling over as his hungover body lacked any sense of balance. Luckily, the coffee table stopped him from falling off the couch, his shins knocking into the wood with a sharp smack.

Cursing the table, Dean hobbled down the hallway to the bathroom. His shins still throbbed by the time he was washing his hands, and it did nothing to improve his hangover-induced bad mood. Making his way out of the bathroom, he shuffled into Sloane's kitchen and began brewing the coffee. He stopped short when he saw the coffeemaker wasn't prepped, but not to be deterred from his morning cup, Dean tossed the water and grounds in and slapped the button.

Rubbing his head against the pulsing throb deep in his skull, he made his way back to the living room. Dean stopped short as he saw their glasses and Sloane's half-finished beer were left out, as was the bottle of vodka. It looked like any other drunken night the two of them had engaged in on the rare occasion, right down to the burger wrappers balled up and left on the table.

But last night hadn't been like any other drunken night.

Dean closed his eyes as the previous night's events rushed back to him. He covered his face, forcing himself to take a deep, steadying breath. There had been a few instances of next morning regrets, but none had turned his stomach quite like remembering what he'd done with Sloane.

"Oh God," Dean groaned.

A thump drew him around, and he whirled to face the sound. Immediately, he regretted the decision as the room spun, forcing him to grip the nearby chair to stay upright. The sudden shot of pain through his skull he could live with, but the sight of Sloane standing at the end of the hallway was something he wasn't ready for.

"Hungover?" Sloane asked with a rasp.

Hungover and almost panicking, but Dean simply nodded. He was more than aware that despite typically only pulling on a pair of pants or shorts when he woke up, Sloane had dressed fully before emerging from his room. And Dean didn't like how Sloane wasn't looking him in the eye for more than a few seconds.

"Drank enough to regret it," Dean said.

Sloane nodded, continuing his path to the kitchen. He glanced at Dean as he passed, and Dean wondered if Sloane was purposefully keeping his distance or if he was just imagining it.

"Oh, you got it going," Sloane said as he stopped in the kitchen doorway.

Dean nodded. "You know me, got to have my cup."

Sloane grunted. "Right, you have your shift today."

Dean blinked, turning around to try and find his phone. In the wake of his hangover and the realization of what they'd done, Dean had almost completely forgotten about his upcoming shift at the clinic. A weird mixture of relief and disappointment flooded through him when he saw he still had another hour before he had to leave.

"Running late?" Sloane asked.

Was that hope in his voice?

Dean shrugged. "I woke up early, I guess. Never sleep very well when I drink too much."

"You don't normally drink that much," Sloane noted.

Dean glanced at him and found he couldn't read his friend's expression. It could just be the hangover Sloane was possibly feeling, or more likely, Sloane was just as freaked out by what had happened as Dean. If it was the second case, Dean couldn't blame him, and he was more surprised Sloane was even bothering to talk to him.

"I guess it got out of hand," Dean admitted.

Sloane said nothing, chewing his bottom lip as he watched Dean.

Dean was the first to look away, unwilling to endure Sloane's thoughtful but distant expression anymore. How had he gone from years of keeping his secret to blabbing it in the heat of a moment and then pushing himself onto Sloane? How Sloane wasn't mad, frustrated, or even outright upset was a puzzle to Dean, but he hated the silence stretching between them.

Sloane glanced in the kitchen. "I think your coffee is ready."

"Not going to have any?" Dean asked.

Sloane shook his head. "Just getting a bottle of water and going back to bed."

Which required him to get dressed first, of course. Dean closed his eyes, shaking his head as he tried to ignore his heart pounding. If he let himself think too much about what happened and what was going on, he would lose his mind. They had been so close to getting things back to normal, and then he'd thrown it all away in a moment of drunken impulsivity.

Sloane looked him over, a frown creasing his brow. "Dean."

Dean shook his head, giving a laugh he didn't feel. "I think I'm going to head out and get things set up. Weekends are always the busiest."

Sloane hesitated and then nodded. "Alright, if that's what you want."

Dean almost laughed again, knowing Sloane had to be relieved to see Dean go. He did, however, force a smile as he gathered the bottles and the glasses to clean up before he left. Sloane shuffled out of his way as Dean hurried into the kitchen. With that done, he grabbed the travel mug he always left at Sloane's and filled it with coffee.

"Text me later?" Dean asked brightly as he yanked on his boots.

Sloane nodded as he retreated to his bedroom, the bottle of water in hand. "Yeah, don't forget to eat."

The casual, friendly reminder should have made him feel better, but instead, Dean took it like a stab to the gut. It had sounded so perfunctory, a product of habit, and Sloane still hadn't looked at him.

Maybe he would volunteer for a double shift.

* * *

THE SMELL of something spicy and rich brought his head up. Sniffing at the air, Dean turned in his chair to find Troy standing in the doorway. The man was smirking, holding a plastic bag as he waited.

Dean eyed it. "What's that?"

Troy wiggled it. "For you, if you're good."

Dean's stomach rumbled, but he eyed his friend warily. "Define good."

"You eat it and stop being so weird."

Dean frowned. "I'm not being weird."

Troy raised a thin brow. "Right, because normally, when you're hungover, you're a grumpy shit. But you've been hungover the whole shift and haven't growled at me once."

"You...want me to be grumpy?"

"I want you to stop acting weird."

Dean looked at the bag again. "Is that curry?"

"Might be."

"From India's Delights?"

"Could be."

"Troy," Dean growled in warning.

Troy grinned, holding out the bag. "There we go."

Dean snatched the bag, mouth watering as he yanked out the takeout container and slapped it on his desk. He'd been wondering how he would get through another shift without eating, and now the answer had been dropped in his lap. Maybe he wouldn't regret volunteering to work a double after all.

Troy plopped himself down on Dean's desk. "So, what's up with you anyway?"

Dean shoved a forkful in his mouth, moaning as the spice lit up his tongue. He eyed Troy, shrugging as he gathered another mouthful.

"Shoving food in your mouth isn't going to save you from my questions," Troy said.

"But I can try," Dean noted.

"You not get any sleep again?" Troy asked.

"I sleep," Dean protested.

"Yeah, and sometimes you go through stretches of sleeping like total shit."

That was true, but Dean hadn't known it had been obvious to anyone but Sloane and maybe Marco. Usually, when his sleep was disrupted by the nightmares of his last mission before returning to the States, he retreated to Sloane's. Dean wasn't sure if Sloane knew Dean slept better when he stayed in his apartment, surrounded by the man's presence and even the faint hint of his cologne, but he never questioned when Dean showed up without warning to crash on his couch.

Dread settled in his gut, and Dean realized the night before had been the first time he'd slept poorly at Sloane's.

"You and Sloane get into it again?"

Dean choked on his food. "Excuse me?"

Troy snorted. "It's obvious you two had some sort of falling out before. I thought you being quiet today meant you two had talked, but you've just been weirdly quiet."

True, Dean hadn't exactly felt sociable, but he didn't think that was so odd. He could easily go through a shift without needing to socialize, but Troy usually ensured that he did. The more he thought about it, the more he realized he had been unusually clipped in his conversations with Troy.

"No, we didn't fight," Dean said truthfully.

"Things not work out with you and Marco?" Troy guessed.

Dean cringed, really wishing Troy would stop. The last thing he wanted to think about was Marco while trying to make sense of what he'd done. True, he and Marco were still in the casual dating stage, but it didn't make Dean feel any better. Not that he felt as though he had crossed a line. He was safe in that regard, if only because he'd been too afraid to commit to Marco yet. But if he was still so hung up on Sloane that he was willing to give the guy head in the heat of the moment without a second thought, what did that say about the possible longevity of a potential relationship with Marco?

"Nothing happened with Marco," Dean said finally.

Troy eyed him, smiling. "You gonna tell me anything?"

"You're being nosy."

"I'm concerned. You've been in a foul mood forever, and apparently, Sloane has too. Now you show up today, and you're practically on a different plane of existence."

Dean pushed his food around, chewing slowly as he considered what to say. Troy might be chatty, but Dean knew he wouldn't blabber to everyone who might listen. The two of them worked well together for a reason, and Dean had come to trust the man.

But the idea of telling the whole story filled him with dread.

Dean sighed. "We're not...fighting, but things are really strained with Sloane and me at the moment."

"Because?"

Dean looked up, wincing apologetically. "Would you blame me if I said I don't want to get into it?"

Troy cocked his head, then sighed. "Alright, then, what will you tell me?"

Dean frowned. "We were fighting before. That's why I was in such a bad mood."

"Right, I already figured that out on my own."

"And last night, we kind of got over it?"

"Kind of."

"We agreed we wanted to be friends again and deal with

the fight when we weren't acting like idiots."

Troy laughed. "One of these days, I want a friendship like you two have."

"Dysfunctional and stupid?" Dean asked.

"You're both idiots, but you're idiots who get along perfectly. You know how many friends I've had who let our friendship go over one fight? You two had a fight and were miserable shits for over a week, and then you meet up and just want to move on."

Dean raised a brow. "Shouldn't you be telling me that it's not healthy to ignore what caused the fight?"

Troy shook his head. "Why? Not every argument has to be something you need to talk about. Sometimes, talking about every little problem is what causes more problems. If you two need to talk about it, then do it. Otherwise, who gives a shit? Better to be back to being friends and deal with it when you're calm and have thought about it."

Dean grunted. "I guess that was our thinking."

"Plus, if it stops you from constantly being a snarky asshole, I'll take it."

Dean glared at him. "Thanks."

Troy winked. "I much prefer you happy and not so miserable you look like you hate everything, Dean. You and Sloane are probably the best duo I've ever seen, and he actually seems happy around you."

Dean snorted softly, staring down at his cooling food. "Don't know if that's the case anymore."

"Is this where you don't tell me what's caused this new problem?"

Dean shrugged, refusing to look up. "I...went too far with something. Definitely pushed over the line, and now we're both just...well, I wouldn't blame him for hating me."

Troy hummed, his finger tapping on the desktop. "Just enough detail to make me curious about the rest."

Dean sighed. "Troy."

"I won't, don't worry. Look, I won't even try to guess what you're talking about because that's asking for trouble. What I will say, though, is that you need to stop overthinking it."

"And if I have good reason for it?" Dean asked.

"You always think you do, but that doesn't make you right. Just...look, the man's your best friend, and he's not going to hate you. Unless you, like, hurt his family or something, then yeah, but otherwise? It's obvious to anyone who's been around you two that there's something special there."

Dean looked up sharply. "Something special?"

Troy chuckled. "I'd be lying if I said I hadn't wondered if there was more going on with you two than you let on."

Dean's eyes widened. "What?"

"Stop, it's just a thought. Don't get me wrong, you two would be a cute couple, and sometimes I still wonder, but you guys are what you are. Ultimately, that's all that matters, and you shouldn't worry too much. Sloane's a stubborn jerk, and you're just as hardheaded. You guys aren't going to fall apart that easily."

"You really thought something was going on with us?" Dean asked.

Troy screwed up his face in thought. "Weird, but not on your end. On his, though? Yeah, I have."

"You thought the straight guy had something going for me?" Dean asked incredulously.

Troy shrugged. "Call it a hunch, call it idle fantasy, I don't know."

Dean rolled his eyes, jabbing Troy with the plastic fork. "Now we're getting into your weird fantasies. It's time to call this meeting to an end."

"Hey," Troy protested, wiping his arm.

A deep voice cleared its throat behind them, and Dean

turned in his chair. A dark-haired man with even darker eyes stared at them, turning his gaze from Dean before locking back on Troy. Dean didn't think he'd seen the man before, looking him over.

The man nodded toward Dean. "Sorry to interrupt."

Dean looked down, catching sight of the spot where the soldier's hand should have been. Instead, there was just a loose sleeve.

"Oscar?" Troy asked quietly.

"Yeah. Hi, Troy."

Dean glanced between them, his brow slowly rising. "You two...know each other?"

Troy tore his gaze from Oscar. "Knew."

The lines on Oscar's face deepened, looking pained. "General Winter told me I needed to come here for a checkup before going on duty."

Dean looked between them again before pointing at Troy with his fork. "He'll get you all set up and checked out."

Troy whirled on him, eyes wide. "What?"

Dean pointed down at his takeout container. "I'm at lunch."

"That I bought you!"

"And I'm so grateful that I want to finish it before it gets cold."

Troy's eyes narrowed. "You—"

Dean winked. "I know."

He had no idea what was going on in his cubicle, but he knew an opportunity when he saw one. It was hard to tell if Troy was really unhappy or if he was just thrown off balance. However, Dean knew it was better for his friend to deal with the situation rather than let it fester, so he shooed him off.

As he turned back to his food, shifting it around carefully, Dean wondered how long it would be until he took his own advice.

SLOANE

Sloane reached out, snatching the phone from Simmons' hand. "Go do a perimeter check."

John blinked at him. "What'd I do?"

Sloane slapped Simmons' phone on the desk. "Driving me crazy."

"How's that different from any other day?"

Sloane pointed at the door with a growl. "Go."

Simmons huffed, pushing out of his seat. "Jesus, fine. Maybe you can stop being a fucking asshole by the time I come back."

Sloane opened his mouth and slammed it shut. The last thing he needed was to lose his shit with John Simmons. The man was a royal pain in the ass, but he didn't deserve to catch the flak for something that had nothing to do with him.

Not that Sloane had any other outlet to funnel his emotions. Not that he knew exactly what his emotions were. He'd been sitting on his thoughts for over a day, and Sloane still had no idea where he stood on what had happened.

The night was crystal clear in his mind, and without the blurring effects of alcohol tilting his thoughts, he understood

I'M STRAIGHT, RIGHT?

precisely what they'd done. Without thinking, pulled by the heat of the moment, Sloane had encouraged Dean to do what they shouldn't have done.

If it had been anyone else, Sloane wasn't sure he would have been torn. He considered himself completely comfortable in his sexuality while still being open-minded. He knew that other perfectly straight men dipped their toes into the waters of different sexuality. Experimentation was pretty normal in his book; he'd just never done it before.

But it couldn't just be experimenting with Dean, not him. There was too much on Dean's end for it to be so shallow and fleeting. Dean had laid his heart bare to Sloane, and how had Sloane repaid him? By letting him give him a blowjob and then not knowing how to react the next day like he was some casual fling from the bar.

But what exactly was it?

It was a question that had been echoing through Sloane's thoughts since he'd woken with a headache and a nauseated stomach. He'd tried to get through the usual morning conversation with Dean, his gut twisting in knots the whole time. Dean had fled, and Sloane hadn't stopped him, not knowing how to make it better or go away.

The question was, did he want it to go away?

Simmons stomped back in, glowering at Sloane as he snatched up the checklist near the door. Sloane watched him, wondering how he was going to apologize to Dean.

He was saved from further introspection by the buzzing of a phone. Heart pumping hard, Sloane reached out to take the phone, praying it was Dean. They had been radio silent for over twenty-four hours now, and Sloane couldn't take another dose of their not talking. He swiped the screen, bringing the message up and freezing.

"Uh," Sloane sputtered.

The message was a picture and not the sort Sloane could

say he'd ever had sent to his phone. In full view of the camera was a man, his ass pointed toward the screen and his legs spread. Below it was a message, racy enough to bring Sloane's brow up, which was only furthered by the last message above, sent by the phone he had in his hand.

"This...is not my phone," Sloane realized aloud.

A strangled cry from behind him brought his head up in time to see a blur moving toward him. The phone was snatched from his hand, and Simmons clutched it to his chest. Wide-eyed, Sloane looked from the phone to Simmons' panic-stricken face.

"Why are you looking at my messages?" Simmons demanded.

Sloane blinked. "I...wasn't thinking, thought it was mine."

He'd forgotten he'd taken John's phone from him before sending the man out to do a perimeter check and had set it on the desk beside him. Without thinking, he'd opened the phone and got more than he expected.

"Why wasn't it locked?" Sloane asked.

"You don't lock yours," Simmons retorted.

True, but then again, he didn't get messages where he would care if someone else saw them, which was more than he could say for Simmons.

Sloane looked him over, finally speaking slowly. "So, that was uh—"

"An accident!"

"An accident."

"Yes."

"Some guy accidentally sent you a nude."

Simmons' fingers tightened over his phone. "My name is...similar to someone else's on his phone."

"And you know that without telling him what happened?" Sloane asked, choosing not to mention Simmons's message before the picture came in.

"It was an accident," John repeated.

Sloane smiled. "John?"

"Don't."

He sighed. "Look, you should know that I, of all people, won't...judge you for that. I mean, look at my best friend."

Simmons looked at his phone. "I'm not."

Sloane remembered Dean telling him how hard it had been for him to accept his sexuality in the beginning. How Dean had tried any number of mental tactics to convince himself he wasn't gay. About how Dean had insisted his interest in the male body was purely curiosity, that it was just hormones playing tricks on him, and any number of hurdles he could think of not to accept the truth. Sloane had found it amusing, coming from Dean's mouth as his friend recounted all the ridiculous ways he'd avoided it.

Seeing Simmons clutching his phone to his heaving chest, sweat breaking out on his forehead, Sloane couldn't see the humor. Sloane reached out, hesitating when Simmons drew his phone further away before finally resting his hand on the man's upper arm.

Sloane took a deep breath. "John, I'm not going to say you are or aren't something, okay? I'm just going to tell you that...if you feel a certain way, there's a reason for it. Maybe you've been feeling it for a while, or maybe it's something new, but don't run from it, man. You'll only end up tired and miserable."

Simmons looked down at Sloane's hand, shaking his head. "It's not that easy."

"Of course it's not. It can be hard to make peace with something unfamiliar, but that doesn't mean you shouldn't."

Simmons looked at him. "What would you know about it?"

Sloane frowned, realizing John had a point...and maybe *he*

didn't. Wasn't his mind filled with doubts, fears, worries, and wonder? Was he giving Simmons advice, or himself?

Sloane gave him a squeeze. "Look, I won't tell you to talk to me. I'm just saying you don't have to run from it, and you should get comfortable with yourself, whoever the hell you are, okay? And fuck, if you need to talk about it, you can."

"With you?" Simmons asked incredulously.

Sloane gave him a pat, chuckling. "Yeah, man. You're an annoying shithead sometimes, but you're not a bad guy."

"Just annoying."

Sloane smirked, digging around for his phone. "Yeah."

"That's the closest to a compliment you've ever gotten with me."

"Yeah, don't tell Trisha, though."

"She'd never believe me."

Sloane chuckled, tapping out a message to Dean before he could second-guess himself. He wasn't going to let this silence stretch out between them again, not this time. Sloane didn't know what the result would be, but he messaged Dean and asked him to meet Sloane at his apartment when their shift was over.

Simmons plopped down in his seat, holding his phone still. "I...thank you."

Sloane glanced sidelong at him, smirking. "Don't worry about it."

"And I...if I want to, I'll talk...to you."

Sloane looked down at Dean's *'ok'* message and smiled sadly. "Good."

* * *

HE'D JUST STEPPED through his door when he stopped, spotting Dean in the hallway. Sloane cocked his head, looking at Dean's untucked shirt, the wild state of his hair,

I'M STRAIGHT, RIGHT?

and the bright, nervous light in his eyes. Sloane didn't know how long Dean had been there, but he'd obviously been losing his mind.

"Dean, what are you doing?" Sloane asked as he closed the door behind him.

Dean took a deep breath, walking up to Sloane. "I can't do this."

Sloane blinked. "Do what?"

Dean shook his head. "This...this quiet, awkward, not talking thing. I can't live knowing I fucked up, that this all went to hell because of me."

Sloane yanked his coat off, tossing it over the back of the chair with a careless gesture. "Dean, hold on."

Dean's lip trembled. "No, Sloane. I can't do this; I won't. I always told myself I was so goddamn lucky to have a friend like you. I never had any real friends growing up, not until I went to basic and met you. You're the best goddamn thing that's happened to me, and I was okay. I was glad to have that, and I was even overjoyed. I don't—"

Sloane watched in frozen horror as Dean's eyes swam, spilling over into a single tear.

"I can't let that all get ruined because of some stupid crush, because of one goddamn drunken night where I was an idiot. I don't care what it takes, Sloane. I'll do whatever it takes to make it up to you. I don't have anyone, I never had any family, I lost my team, and I can't lose you too."

Sloane stared, his arms locked at his side as he watched Dean unravel in front of him. The tears were flowing freely now, and despite the panic in his voice, Dean was still clear and desperate. His shoulders shook, and he seemed unable to keep his arms still as he paced back and forth.

And what was that about his team?

Dean clenched his eyes shut, chest heaving. "I know I fucked up, Sloane. I know I went too far, and I'm *sorry*."

Dean's voice shattered on that final word, and Sloane saw his legs wobble. Ripping himself out of his stupor, Sloane lunged forward, wrapping his arms around Dean. The strength ran out of Dean completely, and he went loose in Sloane's arms.

"I'm sorry," Dean repeated.

Sloane shook his head, allowing Dean to collapse to the ground, safely held in Sloane's arms. Seated on the floor, Dean burrowed himself into Sloane's chest and let out a heartbreaking sob. Sloane wrapped him tighter in his arms, saying nothing as Dean cried his heart out, soaking Sloane's undershirt with his tears.

He didn't know how long he sat there, clutching one of the strongest people he knew, who had finally reached the end of his tether. Sloane knew it was just the weirdness and tension between them that had brought Dean to this point. Dean's fingers dug into Sloane's shoulders, pushing his face closer to his chest as he mumbled and cried to himself.

Little by little, Dean's sobs broke into soft hiccoughs. Sloane ran a hand over his back, letting Dean push himself back so he could sit upright. Dean looked up toward the ceiling, taking a deep breath and closing his eyes before he spoke.

"Shortly after you returned to the States, the team I was with was sent out on a snatch-and-grab. All we needed to do was find the target, grab him, and get out. Simple, easy, the intel said we were clear to go without any issues. They were wrong."

Dean opened his eyes, looking at Sloane with the most haunted expression he'd ever seen on the man's face.

"Someone dropped the ball, or maybe the enemy just found out. Either way, they were waiting for us and caught us when we came through an abandoned village. We fought, but they had us outnumbered, and they knew the area.

Williams was down before we knew what was happening. He took a bullet right through the throat. Dragged him to cover, but he bled out while I tried to staunch the bleeding."

Sloane watched, still holding him by the arms but no longer having to clutch onto him. Dean's eyes had gone hazy as his mind faded into the past.

"Kennig and Heath got caught by an explosion, don't know if it was a mortar or what. It's Kennig I can still hear sometimes when I sleep. He didn't go as quick as Heath. But I think most of all, I remember Mathews. Hit five times as we were retreating to the extraction point. He bled out on the copter on the way back. They said they had to drag me off him, drug me up, but I don't remember."

Sloane gently wiped a tear from Dean's face as his friend continued to sit still, his body drained. Dean blinked at the touch, looking down at Sloane's hand like he'd never seen it before. Dean closed his eyes, leaning his face forward until it rested, cupped in Sloane's hand.

"I never thought I'd be able to tell the story again," Dean whispered.

"I'm sorry," Sloane said, rubbing his thumb over Dean's cheek.

Dean shook his head. "No, it...hurts, but...worth it."

There was nothing he could do to make Dean's pain go away, but Sloane had known that from the moment he'd realized something else was wrong with Dean. The one thing he could do besides being there for his friend was to assuage his other fears.

"Dean," Sloane said softly.

Dean's eyes flashed open, shifting to Sloane's face warily. "Yeah?"

Sloane smiled, giving Dean's cheek a gentle squeeze. "You were *never* in danger of losing me, never."

"Even after—"

Sloane shook his head. "Never. I can't tell you where my head is at about that exactly, not right at this moment. I still need a little time to think about it. But when it comes to you, I'm never unsure. Whatever I might feel about what happened, I will always want you to be a part of my life, so long as you want to be."

Dean's lip trembled. "I don't want to lose you."

"I'm not walking away from you, Dean, and I won't push you away either. We'll figure this out once we've had some time to get our heads on straight."

Dean's lips trembled. "Not really all that straight, is it?"

Sloane chuckled, drawing Dean in for another tight hug. "Smartass."

Dean burrowed his face in Sloane's neck, nodding. "Thank you, Sloane."

Sloane sat there, content to hold Dean for as long as the man needed him. He'd told Dean the truth; he didn't know how he felt or where his head was, but he had Dean, and right now, that was enough.

But for Dean's sake, he was going to have to figure it out soon.

DEAN

Dean fumbled with his phone, nearly dropping it on the floor. The clock on the front showed only a couple of minutes had passed, and Dean let out a low sigh. While he was more than confident he was doing the right thing, he was quickly discovering that the idea sounded more noble than it felt.

A knock at his apartment door brought his head up with a snap, followed by a wince. His nerves were stretched tight, and he was already overreacting. Forcing himself to take a deep breath, Dean pushed up from the couch and went to the door. He opened it to find Marco standing there, looking at Dean carefully.

"Hey, Dean," Marco said, waiting in the hallway.

Dean opened the door, inviting him in with a wave. "Hey, come on in."

Marco stepped forward, inching his way inside. Dean saw Marco's bright eyes search his face and then noted how Marco didn't take his shoes off. Not that Dean enforced a no-shoes rule in his apartment, but Marco always had before.

"You can sit," Dean told him with a light laugh.

Marco did, choosing the couch as his spot, and watched Dean intently. It took Dean a moment to realize he should probably sit as well. He hesitated, unsure if he should sit across from Marco or beside him.

Marco smiled, patting the couch. "C'mon and sit, Dean."

Well, they were already off to a bad start. Dean wanted to keep control of the situation, to make it as smooth as possible and with the least pain or struggle. While he wasn't surprised that Marco knew something was going on, Dean hated that he was already making a botch of it by bumbling.

Dean did sit, though, and took a deep breath. "I...wanted to talk to you."

"I gathered as much."

Dean took a deep breath, nodding. After everything that happened, Dean knew what he needed to do. Even if everything with Sloane crashed and burned, Dean knew it wasn't right to continue things with Marco. They might not have committed to one another yet, but Dean knew he owed Marco a clean break.

It sucked, and Dean hated it. He really liked Marco, and if perhaps the situation had been different, Dean might have fallen for him given time. The man was wise beyond his years, patient, and had just the right amount of playfulness, which brought a smile to Dean's face. Yet, in the end, Dean would never be able to follow through on anything with Marco so long as the specter of Sloane hung over him. So long as the possibility existed, he could never give Marco what he deserved.

Marco smiled, placing a hand gently on Dean's jaw. "Dean...it's okay."

Dean shook his head, trying to force himself to speak. He needed to get the truth out before he lost his nerve. All the speeches he'd practiced were gone, and he found the words slipping from him.

"It's not," Dean insisted.

He clenched his eyes shut, forcing himself to take a deep breath. If it hadn't been obvious to Marco that Dean hadn't called him to give him good news, Dean knew it had to be now. Dean could barely get his mouth to open, and it felt dryer than the desert in there.

"I already know," Marco said softly.

Dean's eyes flew open, nerves gone in a cold splash of surprise. "What?"

"You and Sloane?"

Dean blinked. "I...but—"

Marco chuckled. "I kind of...wondered after the first few times you talked about him."

Dean shook his head. "But nothing was going on."

"Maybe not on his end, but I thought there might be something on yours. Just the way you spoke about him, there was something in your eyes that said maybe, just maybe, there was more than friendship going on there."

Dean's fingers unclenched, going limp in his lap. "But...you never said anything? It didn't bother you?"

Marco rubbed the back of his head. "We all go into relationships and dating with baggage attached, Dean. That's something you learn to accept when seeing someone new. By the time I suspected it, I'd already gotten to know you a bit. And sure, part of it was that I really do like you, so I was willing to look past it. Thing is, I also figured out you were the sort of person that if you were trying to date someone, you were probably okay to date."

Dean looked down at his hands, shaking his head. "I guess you were wrong on that one, huh?"

"I wouldn't say I was wrong. After all, the time I've spent with you has been wonderful, and it's a shame I couldn't have had more. But I can't fault you for being in love with him."

Dean looked up, snorting. "Really? After the way he behaved with you?"

Marco raised a brow. "Yeah, about that. That was my other clue that something else was going on. I mean, I get the overprotective best friend thing, and even being grumpy that you were keeping it from him, but he was a bit...much. Sure, he's 'straight' and all, but that most certainly did make me question it."

"I don't even know what he is or...if this is anything worth trying to figure out," Dean admitted.

Marco shook his head. "Trying to figure out what he is or isn't will just hurt both your heads. I don't think there's an easy definition there."

"Definitions help."

"Definitions make some things easier, but trying to force those definitions can make things harder than they need to be. Do you see what I mean?"

Dean frowned. "Not...really."

Marco took his hand. "You'll figure it out. Just don't go focusing too much on labeling things."

"Those labels help if I need to figure out what to do."

Marco blinked. "Figure out what to do? Don't you already have that part figured out?"

Dean laughed. "Do I strike you as someone who knows what the hell they're doing?"

"Didn't you get me to come here to end things with me so you can go full force into a relationship with Sloane?"

"No, I got you to come here to end things with you because it wasn't fair for me to keep seeing you while I have all this figuring out to do. Sloane and I have barely spoken about...that. We have a little, and I know he's thinking about things, but we haven't been able to talk about what's going on between us."

"So, you're avoiding it."

I'M STRAIGHT, RIGHT?

"No!"

"Right, so you're avoiding it, which won't help either of you. Look, just talk to him, okay?"

Dean stared at him in wonder. "Why are you being so nice about this?"

Marco laughed. "What do you mean?"

"I mean, I just...I'm basically ditching you to go figure out things with my straight best friend."

"First of all, as much as I said not to put a label on things, it might be time not to think of him as totally straight, or at least not where you're concerned. Secondly, why would I be mad? On a practical level, we were never committed, so it's not like you've cheated on me and left me for another man. On an emotional level, you have to follow your heart. If that's not with me, it's better to end it now, like you were trying to do. At the end of the day, you have to do what's right for you, Dean, and if trying to figure out things with Sloane is the way you have to go about it, then do that."

Dean snorted softly. "Doesn't feel fair to you."

"What's less fair, being with me when your heart wants someone else? Or letting me down as gently as you can before things get serious? Dean, you're a good guy. The fact that you did this proves that. You obviously have a wonderful thing with Sloane, and it looks like there's a chance for something even more. So, why don't you go and take the damn risk?"

"Quit hemming and hawing, eh?" Dean asked.

"Shit or get off the pot is what I'm saying here."

Dean reached out, squeezing Marco's shoulder. "You're right. And I'm sorry it ended up this way, Marco. I hope you find someone who doesn't have all these hang-ups and can give you what you deserve."

Marco snorted, patting Dean's hand. "Quit worrying

about me. I've got plenty of time for that. Worry about yourself."

Dean didn't know how he was going to, but he supposed it was about time he made a go of it. He and Sloane had been dancing around the entire problem since Dean had spilled his guts. It was time they dealt with the problem head-on. Even if the thought made his stomach flutter hard enough, he feared it might float off.

"And hey, call me and let me know how it goes?" Marco asked.

Dean smiled, bending down to kiss Marco's cheek. "I will, thank you, Marco."

The rest was up to him.

SLOANE

In retrospect, Sloane supposed he might have chosen a better way to greet Dean when he came through the door to his apartment. The problem was that Sloane had been left to his own devices for a couple of days, with minimal conversation from Dean. Guilt and nerves had eaten their way through Sloane's thoughts until all he could think about was what they had said, hadn't said, and what they'd done. By the time he went to Dean's apartment to wait for him so they could find a way to end the madness, Sloane was a living bundle of nerves and impulses.

So when Dean came through the door, Sloane had literally all but jumped the man. Dean, understandably, had not been expecting Sloane and lashed out with a yelp. Pain shot up Sloane's jaw and he stumbled back, holding his face with a muttered curse.

Dean's eyes widened. "Holy shit, Sloane! What the hell are you doing?"

"Learning that you have one hell of a right hook, holy shit is right," Sloane grumbled, rubbing his jaw.

"You scared the hell out of me!"

"Hitting someone when they startle you is new," Sloane said.

Dean blinked, turning to close the door. "Old habits."

Sloane didn't need Dean's distant tone to tell him what the man was thinking. Dean glanced at him, and Sloane could see the shadow of Dean's nightmares again. Sloane reached out, taking hold of Dean's arm and squeezing it gently. Dean gave him a grateful smile, taking hold of Sloane's arm and returning the pressure. They stood there in silence as Dean accepted not only that Sloane finally knew his blood-soaked story, the only other person who did, but the silent comfort Sloane offered him.

Dean drew his hand away. "What are you doing here?"

For a moment, Sloane had to wonder the same thing, distracted by the warmth still lingering where Dean's hand had been. Had he always felt like that after Dean touched him, or was that new? Despite feeling confident in his decision, Sloane still couldn't decide what was different and what he saw differently.

"Sloane?"

He looked up, startled, as he realized he was still staring down at his arm. Dean was watching him, worry heavy in his dark brown eyes. Sloane's chest constricted as he looked Dean in the eye, desperately trying to remember what he was supposed to say.

Sloane cleared his throat. "I...wanted to talk to you."

Dean's gaze was guarded. "That's fair. I guess it's about time we talked. Should I get us something to drink?"

"Umm, is that a good idea?" Sloane asked, his cheeks flushing as he remembered the sight of Dean's face between his legs.

Dean closed his eyes, shaking his head. "I guess not."

"Plus, I'd rather be sober for this anyway," Sloane admitted.

I'M STRAIGHT, RIGHT?

"I'm not sure if that's supposed to make me feel better. And if so, whether or not it's working," Dean said slowly.

Sloane sighed, rubbing his hands over his face as he tried to think about what he wanted to say. The thought sent a ripple of frustration through him since that was all he'd been thinking about for the past couple of days. Everything he'd rehearsed, broken down, and memorized had fled his mind. He was going to end up screwing everything up like he had the last time he'd tried to fix things between him and Dean when all he wanted was to make things right, make them perfect.

Warm fingers slipped into his hand, pulling it away from his face. Sloane opened his eyes, looking down at his hand and then up at Dean. His friend was smiling softly and squeezed Sloane's hand gently.

"It's okay, Sloane," Dean said softly.

"I should be the one saying that to you. You're the one who's been hurt the most by all this," Sloane grumbled.

"It hasn't exactly been a cakewalk for you," Dean said.

Sloane gripped Dean's hand tighter, taking comfort in the familiar contact. "The difference is that I've only been bothered by this whole thing for a while. You've been hurting over this for years, Dean."

Dean smiled sadly. "I can't blame you for being bothered by it, and I was used to it. It's not like it was your fault."

Sloane winced. "I didn't mean I was bothered in like...a bad way. I just—"

He grunted, turning away with a growl of frustration. It was exactly like he'd feared. Nothing was coming out of his mouth right. His family was far better at explaining their emotions than he was at even understanding them. Never had he hated that shortcoming as much as now, when he was trying to figure out how to explain his thoughts to Dean. It felt like everything he said was going to wound Dean more.

"Like, look. Being with you is great, it's wonderful. Shit, even before all this, I said that being around you was better than just about every girl I was with. I'd rather you be the one laying your head on my leg than any girl in the past five years," Sloane said.

Dean chuckled. "I remember you saying once that it was a shame I couldn't give you a blowjob along with the good cuddles."

Sloane cringed. "God, Dean, I'm so sorry."

Dean raised one shoulder and let it drop. "It's okay."

Sloane shook his head. "But it's not."

He reached out, unable to help himself from taking Dean in his grasp again. They were good at talking, and they were good at being around one another, but they had always been at their best when they were touching. Contact between them had always come so easily, and even with everything twisted and confused in his head, Sloane still took great comfort in touching Dean.

The sensation was muddled not only with Sloane's ache over what he'd been inadvertently putting Dean through for years but the memory of their drunken night together. Never once had he looked at Dean in a sexual way. Dean was just Dean to him. Now, though, his mind was filled with the memory of Dean's body pressed against his, the feel of his lips on him, and the sight and sensation of Dean's mouth wrapped around his cock.

Since that night, Sloane had been stuck with the constant nagging feeling of being different. Logically, he knew it had to do with what happened between him and Dean, and despite his conversation with his mother, the reality hadn't completely clicked into place. Now that he was staring Dean in the face, feeling his skin against his, Sloane was starting to understand. Something inside him had flipped, altered, rearranged, or whatever word he thought might apply to the moment.

Dean cocked his head. "Sloane?"

Sloane shook his head. "Look, Dean, I-I don't know how I feel."

"I can understand that. There's been a lot thrown at you."

Sloane sighed. "I can't imagine what it must be like for you."

"I know this isn't what you want to hear, but after nearly six years, I've gotten used to it. Don't give me that look. It's not bad, it means I've had more practice. Plus, I mean, I don't know exactly what's going on in your head right now, but I know you're confused," Dean said.

Sloane looked down at their feet. "I am, but that's not...a bad thing? I mean, you got a little more hands-on with me than usual."

"I did."

"And then you—"

"I did."

Sloane looked up, scanning Dean's face. "And...I liked it."

Dean sucked in a breath. "You did?"

Sloane frowned. "I shouldn't have, you know? I've never thought of any guy like that, and I've definitely never thought about you like that. Hell, whenever someone brought up the idea that you and I might be like that, I just shrugged it off. Come to think of it, I always wondered why it bothered you more, but now I understand."

Dean leaned his face onto Sloane's hand, smiling. "I never realized you noticed. And here I was, thinking I was so subtle."

Sloane watched him, touched by the softness on Dean's face. "I always notice what's going on with you, Dean."

Dean's eyes flashed open, dark in the dim light but full of wonder and warmth. A slow smile spread across his face, and the sight sent Sloane's heart skipping like never before. It was as though, in kissing Sloane, Dean had somehow flipped a switch inside Sloane that he'd never known existed.

"And I meant what I said. I did like what happened, but it's just...jumbled in my head. Like, I shouldn't have liked it, but at the same time, I want more," Sloane said softly.

Dean blinked slowly, hope shining from his eyes. "Yeah?"

Sloane nodded. "I just...don't know how."

Dean chuckled, reaching up to place his hands on Sloane's upper arms. "You're already partway there, big guy. It's just a step further than what we normally do when we spend time together."

Sloane chuckled. "I think it's a few steps further than that."

"You know what I mean."

And Sloane did. In truth, Dean and Sloane had never been afraid to touch, lean against one another, or cuddle. One of Sloane's admittedly short-lived friends with benefits had witnessed him and Dean together while watching a movie. She had stopped by to pick up the tablet she'd accidentally left behind in Sloane's apartment and had found the two of them curled up on the couch. She'd given them an odd look but said nothing, yet Sloane hadn't heard from her again and hadn't thought twice about it.

Sloane stepped forward, bringing his hands down Dean's sides slowly. There was more muscle than Sloane was used to, and none of the curves. Dean sidled closer as he allowed himself to press their bodies together. Again, Sloane noted the difference in how hard Dean was compared to the softness of his previous partners.

Weird as it was mentally, his body stirred to life, albeit with a bit of confusion. While he most certainly wouldn't say he was going to start finding guys worth fucking, some part of him simply translated the confusion to 'it's Dean.' And at the end of the day, that was all that really mattered to him. Angry or happy, hurt or healthy, the fact that he was a guy, Dean was Dean, and Sloane wanted Dean.

Sloane bent his head, pulling his arms tighter around Dean's waist and pressing their lips together. He barely noticed how Dean's lips were firmer than Sloane was used to as a zing of electricity shot through him. For a moment, he was lost between disbelief at what he was doing and surprise at how pleasant the sensation was.

Then, Dean shifted, wriggling his body as he gained a more stable footing, and Sloane's worried thoughts slipped away. Pulling Dean as close as possible, Sloane leaned him back, kissing him even more firmly. Beneath Sloane's touch, Dean's body became firmer yet softer, as though the man was melting against him.

Sloane broke the kiss, letting out a sharp gasp. Dean was staring up at him with a doe-eyed, dazed expression. His cheeks were pink, and his lips were ever so slightly swollen, an indication that Sloane might have kissed him harder than he thought. There was a warmth and a need in Dean's dark eyes Sloane had never seen before, and some deep-seated part of him never wanted Dean to look at anyone else like that.

"Wow," Dean whispered.

Sloane nodded slowly. "Wow, is right."

Dean took a deep breath, letting himself inch back while watching Sloane's face. For a moment, disappointment filled Sloane as he felt Dean's body lose contact with his. Then, it occurred to him that Dean was trying to play it safe, giving Sloane space without demanding too much.

Sloane tightened his grip, keeping Dean still. "I'm not done."

Dean looked at him, one corner of his mouth curling up. "Yeah?"

Sloane nodded. "That was as easy as you said it would be."

Dean's eyes darted over Sloane's face. "But?"

Sloane's heart hammered, and he felt a little lightheaded, but he forced himself to speak, knowing he needed to say the words and knowing he meant them.

"I want to see the rest."

DEAN

His heart beat so ferociously in his chest he thought it was amazing they couldn't hear it. Sloane's words echoed in his head, and Dean swallowed hard, letting them sink in.

How many nights had he lain awake, dreaming of hearing something like that from Sloane? How many fantasies had Dean burned through, thinking what it would feel like to have Sloane hold him, kiss him, mean all of it, and want more?

Dean swallowed. "The rest?"

Sloane's eyes locked on his. "All of it."

Not that Dean didn't want to drag Sloane back to the bedroom immediately, but he knew they had to be careful. Sloane was wandering into territory he wasn't used to, and neither of them was sure what the rules were. Maybe there were none, but Dean didn't want to rush when it might be better to walk carefully.

Dean smiled nervously. "Going from your first kiss with a guy to sleeping with one?"

Sloane's grip tightened. "You're not just a guy. You're you. And last I checked, we already went further than a kiss."

Dean's stomach tightened as he remembered Sloane's pleasure-filled face as Dean slid the man's cock into his mouth. It had been a fantasy realized on its own, but now Sloane was talking about something more than that. Dean didn't care that he would probably be feeling the man's thick cock inside him for days. All he could think about was what it would be like finally to have Sloane.

"Still," Dean said, needing to make sure.

Sloane growled. "Dean."

A shiver ran up Dean's back, and he couldn't help the little gasp. "God, don't do that."

"What?"

"Get all growly and aggressive."

Sloane cocked his head, a shadow of a smirk on his face. "Why?"

Dean narrowed his eyes. "Because."

And just like that, he felt himself propelled backward until his back thumped against the wall. There was no pain, just the sensation of force as his back thumped against it. The shiver of pleasure became a jolt, twisting in Dean's stomach and bringing a low sound from him again.

"Because it turns you on?" Sloane asked, voice low and dangerous.

Holy shit, Dean could actually see pleasure in Sloane's eyes as he realized he was arousing Dean. In all the times he had imagined it and dreamt of what Sloane would look like, Dean realized he had not been ready for the reality. The sight of Sloane, the most heterosexual man Dean had ever known, excited by the idea of turning Dean on, had his knees weak and his breathing sharp.

"Yes," Dean managed, leaning back against the wall.

Sloane pressed his face to Dean's neck, nibbling. "I remember."

Dean's eyelids fluttered. "Remember what?"

"You blowing me."

"Yeah, I remember that. Remembering it even more clearly at the moment."

"And how you liked it when I took over," Sloane said, taking Dean's earlobe between his teeth.

Dean shivered. "Noticed that, huh?"

Sloane's large body pressed against him, pinning him to the wall with a low growl. "I did."

Dean wasn't sure what had changed in the past couple of days, from when Sloane had no idea how he felt about everything to pinning Dean against the wall like he couldn't get enough of him, but hell if he was going to argue. They probably should have talked first. It would have been the reasonable and adult thing to do. But Sloane was holding him tight, nipping at Dean's exposed skin, and Dean could feel the man's huge cock was harder than it had been the night of the blowjob.

He'd be sensible some other time.

Dean turned his head, catching Sloane's mouth with his and pressing firmly into the kiss. Fire lit in his gut, curling up and through his body as his lips parted, welcoming Sloane's tongue. Dean wrapped his arms around Sloane's neck, drawing him in the last inch so he could feel every part of Sloane's powerful muscles bearing down around him.

Sloane pulled from the kiss, panting as he looked at Dean. For one moment, Dean thought Sloane was having second thoughts and he was going to bail. That he realized, despite whatever he thought a moment ago, he was straight, and there was no way this was happening. Then Dean was up in the air, Sloane's thick arms around his waist and dropping Dean onto Sloane's broad shoulder.

Dean gave a startled yelp. "Sloane!"

Sloane chuckled, patting Dean's butt as he turned to walk down the hallway. "Shut up. You love it."

"This is ridiculous," Dean said with a laugh.

"You say, as though I can't feel you hard against my shoulder," Sloane snorted.

Dean glared, leaning down so he could swat Sloane's ass in return. "Not the point."

"So, I shouldn't toss you on the bed and pin you to it while I kiss you?" Sloane asked as he stopped at the edge of Dean's bed.

Dean hesitated, screwing up his face as he realized he was caught. "That's...you're an ass."

Unsurprisingly, Sloane chose to retort by hefting Dean up and letting him drop onto the bed. Dean bounced once before he felt Sloane's weight press down on him, preventing him from bouncing again. Sloane grinned as he hovered over Dean, pinning his arms with each hand and using his weight to keep Dean's lower body in place.

Dean grunted, squirming under Sloane. "Cheat."

Sloane bent down, nipping at Dean's bottom lip. "I'm not going to lie to you; this is...fun to see."

"Me irritated with you? That's nothing new," Dean shot back.

"You irritated, panting, and wanting me to fuck you," Sloane growled in his ear.

"Oh, holy shit," Dean groaned.

Forgetting all about his annoyance, Dean pushed his hips up, trying to get some friction on his straining cock. He had always wondered if Sloane was as dominant and aggressive in bed as he could be in real life, and he was absolutely delighted to find out it was true. That did not, however, make Dean any less desperate for them to get their clothes off.

Sloane released his grip on Dean's wrists before moving his hands down to Dean's shirt. Dean lifted himself up in time for Sloane to yank his shirt over his head. The cool air of his apartment brushed over his skin but was replaced by the warm press of Sloane's hands.

Dean almost protested the gentle touches until he looked at Sloane's face. Written over the man's handsome features was pure wonder. Dean watched him, shivering as Sloane's fingers stroked his sides, over his stomach, and around his chest. Sloane gave an experimental squeeze of Dean's arms before slowly inching his way off Dean's body.

Dean watched as Sloane slid his hands over Dean's waist and down his legs. Sloane took hold of Dean's pants, undoing the button and unzipping them carefully. Dean realized Sloane had probably never undressed a guy before, and it was almost amusing to watch the care he took with the zipper. When Sloane saw Dean had underwear protecting his tender bits, however, he took hold of them and the jeans and pulled them down.

Sloane's eyes roamed over Dean's lower half as he pulled the last of Dean's clothes off completely. Warm hands massaged their way up Dean's legs, gripping his thighs and up over his hips. He waited, watching as Sloane slowly made to take hold of Dean's cock with a firm but careful grip.

"Oof," Dean grunted, unable to help himself.

Sloane looked up. "You okay?"

Dean chuckled deep in his throat. "Oh, better than okay, this is, yeah, I'm definitely okay."

Sloane grinned, running a thumb over the head of Dean's cock. Dean watched, wide-eyed as Sloane bent down, kissing the tip before pulling away and running his tongue over his lips.

"Huh, not what I was expecting," Sloane commented.

Dean almost asked what Sloane meant until he saw the drop of fluid coming from the tip of his cock. He had been leaking, and apparently, during his sweet and incredibly sexy gesture, Sloane had got some on his lips.

"Sorry," Dean said with a light laugh.

Sloane reached down, taking hold of the outline of his own hard cock. "Don't be. This is still here."

With his attention averted, Dean's gaze locked on the bulge. Sloane followed his gaze, smirking as he moved his fingers up to the button of his pants. With far less careful movements, Sloane's pants were undone and began slipping down his waist. Dean watched eagerly as the dark trail on Sloane's stomach became visible inch by inch, revealing a dark patch and then the thickness of Sloane's cock. Sloane stood at the end of the bed, letting his pants fall away, revealing his thick, heavy shaft.

"I almost forgot how big that thing is in person," Dean muttered.

Sloane looked up, concern reaching his eyes. "Uh, we don't have to, you know—"

Dean smiled. "You want to fuck me?"

Sloane chuckled, taking hold of the base of his cock and giving it a squeeze. "I did say *all*."

Dean reached out toward him. "Then, get that shirt off and come here, and let me show you it all."

Sloane did as he was told, shucking off his shirt and tossing it away before climbing onto the bed. Of all the things Dean loved about the moment, he treasured the feel of Sloane's naked, warm body pressing down onto him as he kissed him. Held tight, with Sloane's tongue sliding over his own, Dean felt a wash of pure bliss pass through him.

"God, you feel...good," Sloane whispered, rutting against Dean as he spoke.

Dean chuckled, not taking offense at the slight hesitance in Sloane's words. For a man who was probably used to far softer, curvier bodies, Dean had no doubt Sloane was in a strange place being turned on by Dean. But by God, he was turned on, and Dean shivered as he felt Sloane's stiff cock slide alongside his own.

Dean gave him a light push. "Get on your back."

Sloane hummed, doing so. "Bossy."

Dean chuckled, rolling over to open the bedside table drawer. "You love it."

He snatched the lube and then considered the condoms sitting next to it. Dean had, of course, used them before, and hesitantly, he picked one of the condoms meant for larger sizes. He knew how he felt about the idea, but he turned and held the condom in the air for Sloane's opinion.

Sloane smiled gently at it. "I don't."

Dean grinned, tossing it back into the drawer without hesitation. Even though technically he would have known if Sloane had something, since he had access to the man's medical records, he would have trusted Sloane instantly. And if he were completely honest, the idea of feeling Sloane inside him, bare and unhindered, was exactly the way Dean would have chosen it.

Straddling Sloane's hips, Dean uncapped the bottle of lube and poured a healthy amount onto his hand. Sloane's eyes watched closely, his bottom lip caught between his teeth as Dean reached behind him. Dean let out a low breath as his fingers closed around the thick girth of Sloane's cock, sliding over it to coat it with lube. He took his time, making sure every nook and cranny of the thick shaft was coated and ready for action. He used it as the perfect excuse to grope Sloane.

With that done, Dean leaned forward, propping himself up with his dry hand. With his still slick hand, he pressed one finger against himself. One digit was nothing, and he slid it inside his hole. Dean pressed his mouth against Sloane's chest, kissing him gently as he slid another finger alongside the first.

Sloane's eyes were wide as Dean looked up. "Are you—"

Dean chuckled, letting out a low groan as he nuzzled Sloane's chest, adding a third finger.

"I'm not going into this completely unprepared. You aren't exactly small."

Sloane cupped his face, kissing him as Dean let out another groan. He would probably need more work than he was doing to be completely ready, but Dean wasn't patient enough. Pulling his fingers free, he gripped the base of Sloane's cock and angled it until it pressed against him.

"All of it?" Dean asked as he began to push his hips back.

Sloane reached down, taking hold of Dean's hips. "All of it."

Dean gave that last extra push, body stiffening as Sloane's thick head pushed past the ring of muscle. Below him, Sloane's eyes widened even further, encouraging Dean to push back even more. He couldn't stop the moan that fell from his lips as Sloane's cock spread him wide with every inch. Sloane's fingers dug into his hips, not moving Dean but keeping a fierce grip on him as Sloane's cock filled him.

It took a little more work than Dean expected, and the burning sensation wasn't his favorite, but Dean let out a low, pleasured moan as he pushed the last inch of Sloane into him. Dean was sure Sloane was absolutely the biggest he'd ever had, and if it were anyone else, he might have just stuck with giving him a blowjob.

Sloane's voice shook. "Are you...okay?"

Dean took a deep breath, nodding his head. It was probably the most intense feeling he'd ever had, having someone so thick and long inside him. But it was Sloane, and that was all Dean needed to love every sensation washing through him.

"Fuck, that's good," Dean murmured as he began to move his hips.

Sloane's breath caught, coming out in a stuttering gasp. "Holy shit."

Dean echoed that statement but kept his focus on moving steadily. Each movement pulled and tugged inside him, sparking a whole new degree of sensation and pleasure he hadn't known existed. He could feel himself loosening up as he pushed Sloane's thick cock deep inside with every back thrust of his hips, though. Dean wanted to feel every inch of Sloane, but he desperately wanted to get to the part where it was Sloane taking over, where it was Sloane's hips shoving deep as he ground into Dean.

Sloane huffed, his arms trembling as he fought to keep still. "Dean."

Honestly, he didn't care if he wasn't ready. He'd deal with it.

Dean bent down, kissing Sloane. "Roll us over and fuck me."

Sloane wasted no time wrapping his arms around Dean's waist, thrusting up to the hilt. Dean gasped, head spinning as they rolled, and his back was pressed against the bed. Sloane took a moment to adjust his position, moving his grip to Dean's hips and rearing back. With Dean resting against the bed, Sloane sheathed his cock fully inside him again.

Dean cried out, his hands gripping tight to Sloane's forearms as Sloane's cock spread him open. Sloane hesitated only a moment before catching sight of Dean's panting face and rearing back to thrust in again. At first, his movements were measured and experimental, steadily building in strength as he learned what Dean could handle and what he wanted.

As he continued, Sloane bowed over Dean's body, pinning him to the mattress. Dean's legs wrapped tightly around Sloane's hips, his shoulders pressed to the bed as he continued to grip Sloane's arms. His head spun with pleasure and pure wonder as he watched Sloane piston his hips down into him. Their bodies crashed together with every movement of Sloane's cock inside him, lighting his body up with sheer pleasure and ecstasy.

Sweat beaded on Sloane's forehead as he thrust hard down into Dean's body, low moans and chest-deep groans falling from his lips. His muscles worked and rolled beneath his skin, and Dean watched as Sloane lost himself to the pleasure.

Sloane grunted, forcing himself to lean on one arm so he could use the other to reach between their bodies. Dean panted, crying out when Sloane's strong fingers wrapped around his cock and began stroking him in time with Sloane's thrusts. There was no stopping what was coming, and Dean's body went wild with pleasure as his orgasm crashed around him.

As his body bore down around Sloane, Dean pressed his lips fiercely against his. Sloane gave a surprised grunt, shoving forward one last time as his arm gave out beneath him. On their sides, Dean gripped Sloane even more fiercely, unable to stop the constant flow of groans from his lips as he felt Sloane cum inside him even as he splattered their stomachs with his own orgasm.

As the ecstasy dwindled, Dean was left panting and weak. The acrobatics they had performed began to pull at his muscles, and with a great sense of reluctance, he eased his hips away from Sloane. Beside him, Sloane winced only slightly as he was pulled free from Dean.

"You okay?" Dean asked, stroking Sloane's cheek.

Sloane snorted. "Me? What about you?"

Other than already missing the feeling of Sloane inside him, Dean was perfect. All the times he'd dreamt of being with Sloane, he had never truly known how perfect and divine it would be. Dean had had sex before, and he'd had amazing sex, but nothing compared to the feeling of Sloane

I'M STRAIGHT, RIGHT?

deep inside him, holding him tight as he thrust with abandon.

"I'm great," Dean told him with a little laugh.

Sloane leaned forward, gently kissing Dean. Laying a finger on Dean's lips, Sloane pushed away and off the bed. Dean watched him go, his heart skipping a beat until he saw Sloane leave the room without taking his clothes. A light came on down the hall, and he heard water. Less than a minute later, the light turned off, and Sloane reappeared in the doorway.

Sloane sat on the edge of the bed, a washcloth in his hand. Dean reached out, but Sloane ignored him, taking it upon himself to wipe the damp cloth gently over Dean's cum spattered stomach. Dean lay on his back, flush with a mixture of emotions that threatened to sting the back of his eyes.

Sloane looked up, smiling shyly. "Was it good?"

Dean reached out, stroking his skin. "You get the top spot by a landslide."

Sloane finished cleaning him, tossing the washcloth in the nearby hamper. "I was going to go with mind-blowing, but I like your way of putting it better."

Dean chuckled, too full of warmth and relief to think of anything witty to say. He was spared, however, as Sloane slid back onto the bed with him. Dean smiled as Sloane pressed himself against Dean, and he rolled onto his side at the man's nudge.

Sloane's strong arms wrapped around his waist, snaking over his stomach so his hand lay on his chest. Dean wrapped his arm around Sloane's, hugging it tightly as he curled back into Sloane's body.

"Thank you," Sloane whispered, voice heavy.

Dean stirred. "For?"

"Being you."

Dean's eyes stung, and his throat felt too tight to say

anything, so he simply nodded instead. He lay there, listening to Sloane's breathing slowly deepen and become steady. Dean turned his head enough to see Sloane's peaceful face as he slipped deeper into sleep and smiled.

For once, he thought he would sleep without a worry or a care in the world. Not so long as he was held in Sloane's arms, where he knew he would always be safe.

SLOANE

Warmth and comfort filled his mind as it slowly shifted its way to consciousness. At ease, his mind sifted through the images and sounds, not focusing on any single image but instead taking in the whole sensation. He felt sated, content, and more at ease than he could remember. A weight pressed against his chest, shifting slightly against his arm.

The movement was enough to drag him out of his drifting haze of thought. Cracking his eyes open, Sloane looked around the familiar room that wasn't his. Frowning, he tried to catch his bearings before realizing he was looking at Dean's room. Posters of terrible action films hung in frames on the wall, with smaller picture frames alongside them. Sloane didn't need to get up to know they were mostly pictures of the places Dean had seen during his time in the service. The pictures of Sloane and Dean were in the living room, with one hung beside the plush bed Dean had spent good money on.

His wandering mind snapped back to the present, as everything came crashing back to him. Sloane picked his head up, looking down at the weight against him. Dean slept peacefully, one arm wrapped around the arm Sloane had draped over him, his chest rising and falling slowly.

Sloane had been around Dean while the man slept several times, but he couldn't remember ever seeing him so at peace. He realized Dean looked so much younger in the morning light, especially without the constant furrow that seemed to live on his brow since he'd returned from deployment.

Had Sloane really been the cause of that?

Sloane twisted carefully, looking at the clock. He'd woken a full half-hour before he was supposed to leave for his shift. Relaxing, he rolled back, giving Dean's body a gentle squeeze so as not to wake him.

The night before should have been the strangest of Sloane's life, and in some ways, it still felt a little odd. Sloane had never dreamt of being with a man before and had no interest in the male body. He could certainly understand someone finding a guy attractive and didn't flinch away from admitting when a guy was hot, though he felt none of the attraction himself. Objectively, he had always known Dean was good-looking, well-built, with rugged yet somewhat softened features and brown eyes that were darker than most.

Yet, ever since the night they had drunkenly fallen together, with Dean's lips wrapping around him and opening a door Sloane had never known existed, Sloane saw Dean differently. After that, he could see how much Dean's eyes lit up, burning with emotion and smoldering with passion. He could see and feel the pleasure of just how dexterous Dean's hands could be, and something deep in his gut churned to feel the man's skin pressed against his.

And the night before had just been...something else.

Sloane pressed his nose to the back of Dean's head, breathing deep as he kissed the man gently. It was odd how comforting Dean's sleeping body felt against him. Dean's touch had always been a source of comfort, but now, Sloane felt something far warmer wash through him, mingling with a desire for Dean he'd never felt before.

"I'll be back," Sloane promised the sleeping man.

Careful not to wake Dean, Sloane extracted his arm from around Dean's hips, letting his fingers drift over them. It was a chore not to wake Dean, to see the sleepy expression in his eyes as he came to and saw Sloane. But Sloane kept his hands to himself, making sure Dean was covered before setting his feet on the ground. It was the most peaceful sleep he'd ever seen Dean have, and Sloane couldn't bear to interrupt it.

He was aware of what his absence would say to Dean, though. After carefully pulling his clothes on for his shift, Sloane searched for paper and a pen. Thankfully, Dean relied on old-fashioned handwriting, saying it helped him remember things. It took only a couple of minutes before Sloane found the supplies and jotted down a quick note.

Ripping the note from the pad, he folded it up and made to set it on the table beside Dean's bed. Hesitating, he wrote a quick sentence on the front of the folded letter and began looking for Dean's pants. Once he'd found them, he fished Dean's phone out and plugged it into the charger behind the letter.

Smiling, he bent down to kiss Dean's cheek. "Talk to you in a little bit."

* * *

"You're very quiet," Simmons noted.

Sloane looked up with a smirk. "Not everyone needs to fill the silence by talking all the time."

Simmons eyed him warily. "Yeah, but normally, you're quick to tell me to shut the fuck up and quit bitching."

"You haven't been bitching," Sloane pointed out.

Simmons blinked and then shrugged. "Guess I don't have anything to bitch about."

Sloane cocked his head. "That mean you've been thinking about what we talked about?"

"Is that what you're calling it? Talking?"

Sloane chuckled. "Alright, I told you how it was, and you stared at me like I was the second coming, better?"

"It wasn't...alright, maybe it was."

Sloane waited. "Well?"

Simmons fiddled with the button on his jacket. "I've thought about it, yeah."

Sloane raised a brow. "And?"

"I don't know."

Sloane thought about it before nodding. "That's fair."

Simmons looked up warily. "Is it?"

"Yeah, man, you don't know, but it means you're working on it. That's the first step to figuring shit out, even if that shit is your own. Just...don't run from it, alright? You'll get there, and when you do, wherever it is, you'll be a lot happier."

Simmons stared. "Are...are you giving me good advice?"

Sloane snorted. "Look, if you're a lot happier, you'll bitch less, which means I don't have to listen to it as much. We all win."

"Of course, there's an ulterior motive," Simmons said with a laugh.

Sloane winked. "Welcome to the military."

"Alright, well, I'll keep thinking about it. When I do, would you mind helping me figure it out?" Simmons asked, not quite looking Sloane in the eye as he asked.

Sloane smiled. "Yeah, man, you got it."

Simmons looked up, then away. "Alright, well, your shift ended five minutes ago. Get out of here before Trisha comes in and thinks something's up."

"Yeah, God forbid she thinks you're an actual person," Sloane grunted as he stood up.

He left Simmons with a chuckle, content to let the man sort through things on his own. Sloane knew all too well what that was like, and even still, he was trying to make sense of the conflicts bouncing around in his skull. He knew where it would inevitably lead, but along the way, he was going to have to stop occasionally and figure some things out.

Sloane pulled his phone out, reading the text Dean had sent.

Saw your note. Sure, you need to think, but if you want to come back here, you're welcome.

Sloane had responded that he would be coming back when his shift was over, and after that, silence had fallen between them. That was okay in Sloane's book, even if part of him hated that Dean would be fretting the whole time. He needed to address the frequent texts from his mother while he'd been working, demanding he text her back.

Instead, he swiped on her name, dialing her number. It rang half a dozen times, and just before he was preparing his voicemail speech, her voice came over the line.

"And here I thought you'd forgotten about me."

Sloane snorted. "We both know that's not happening anytime soon."

"Not that you'd think any different. Here I am, worrying about what's going on after the last time you called me, and then you turn around and go silent for two weeks."

Sloane stopped, groaning. "Oh shit, it has been two weeks, hasn't it?"

"Yes, Sloane, it has. I'm going to assume everything worked out."

Sloane looked up, thinking of what to say. "Well, that's one way of putting it."

"Sloane, please tell me you two are not still dancing around each other over one little fight."

Sloane laughed. "No, Mama, we're not. I just meant it didn't quite turn out the way I thought it would?"

"What does that mean?"

Sloane thought about it before deciding where to start. "Well, we made up a few days after I talked to you."

"Which is good."

"Right. It was a little weird, but we made do with one of our hang-out nights. Which turned out pretty good until...things happened."

"Things? What sort of things? Not another fight."

"No, Mama, *things*."

There was a pause followed by, "Oh, things!"

Her stunned voice gave him a laugh. "I'll spare you the details."

"I appreciate that."

"Basically, things happened, and it kind of...threw me off."

"Understandable."

"And things were even more awkward after that."

"Again, I can see why."

"And then I kind of jumped him in his apartment."

"Wait, so...things happened again?"

"Right."

"And you started it that time?"

"Yes."

Sloane could practically hear the wheels in his mother's head spinning as she processed that thought. She might have once commented on how it would have been nice for everyone involved if Sloane was a little less straight, but it had to be different to face that reality. Hell, Sloane still didn't know what it meant, but he wanted to make sure his mother knew all about it. She had always believed in them being open with one another, and he wasn't going to balk just because he was still a little off-balance.

"You slept with Dean."

Sloane couldn't help the ugly snort he gave at the sheer bluntness. "God! And you say I have no tact."

"I said, slept with, not fucked," she replied dryly.

"Oh, shit, Mama, no."

That made her laugh. "So?"

"Yes."

"When I said how it would be nice if you were into Dean, I want you to know that wasn't a dare."

Sloane arched a brow. "You have a problem with this?"

"Don't you pull that one on me, Sloane, you and I both know I'm going to love you no matter who you're sleeping with or who you're dating. But as far as I know, you've never touched another man like that in your life."

"You'd be right."

"And while you've always been…remarkably close to Dean, you were always firmly in the heterosexual camp."

"Again, correct."

"So, this is new territory for you. Which is one thing, but this involves your best friend's heart."

Sloane nodded, agreeing even though she couldn't see it. That fact was the one thing that had kept Sloane from acting sooner. He was so caught up in trying to make sure he didn't hurt Dean any more than he already had that he kept himself immobile and afraid to act. Eventually, he'd lost patience with himself and went with the part of himself that called the loudest.

Cue the best night of intimacy he'd ever had, and he could easily claim the best sex as well.

"Mama, you know I'm not going to hurt him."

"I know, I'm just worried. I didn't see Dean much when he was here, but I liked him. Bit on the quiet side, but God help me, when I found you two curled up together, I prayed you would never lose one another."

Sloane straightened. "Wait, you saw that?"

When Sloane had brought Dean home with him for Easter, the two of them had ended up on the couch watching late-night movies. Sloane's sisters and mother had already gone to sleep, and the two men had enjoyed the comforts of home curled up on the couch. As always happened whenever he and Sloane were close, Dean had ended up pressed against Sloane, soaking in his warmth. They had fallen asleep like that, waking up a few hours later and deciding it was time for them to go to bed.

"I went to get a snack, Sloane, and found you two. It was the first time I ever thought how cute you two looked."

Sloane stopped walking, glancing at his phone in bewilderment. "You thought we were cute?"

"You're so damned stubborn about being affectionate to people. Of course, you show it in your own way, but just outright affection? I rarely see it, but I saw it the night you two were huddled up on the couch."

Sloane shook his head. "A lot of people thought there might be something going on between us."

"If it makes you feel any better, I didn't. I just thought you'd found one of those rare friends that some people never get to meet. The kind of friend who brings out the best in you and brings as much to the table for you as you do for them. Soulmates aren't just romantic, you know."

Sloane laughed softly. "That would have been helpful to hear earlier if I'd ever been worried about feeling so close to him as just friends."

"Well, you've certainly stepped out of the friend zone on this one."

"Oh, yeah."

"So, how *do* you feel?"

And there was the million-dollar question. Where once, being asked how he felt about Dean would have been easy and simple, Sloane found the answer more complex than ever. Did he want Dean close to him for the rest of their lives? Absolutely. Did he want to see Dean smile and laugh and know that Sloane was bringing him happiness? Of course.

But now, Sloane also wanted to see those moments when Dean slept peacefully in his arms. Now, Sloane couldn't help but remember the rumbling moans of pleasure Dean had made when Sloane was deep inside him or the look of pure ecstasy when Sloane had bottomed out in him. Sloane wanted to see Dean as they fell asleep together. When they got ready for work side by side, and while they bitched about their respective jobs.

"I want...what we've always had, but I want...him to be mine?" Sloane said.

"That sounded like a question."

Sloane sighed. "I love Dean. I've loved Dean for years now, and I've never hidden that. But now, it's like that love is...different. I want everything we had before, which I guess already seemed like what you do in a relationship. But I want it in a different way."

There was another pause before his mother finally let out a chuckle. "It sounds like you already know what you're going to do, and you're just telling me."

"I haven't figured out every detail, but I know the general plan."

"Then it sounds like you need to tell Dean that."

Sloane stopped outside Dean's apartment, drawing out the key. "I plan to."

DEAN

Taking a deep breath, Dean sucked in the scent of the salty ocean air. He swore the smell was the only thing keeping him from losing his mind as he watched the waves crash against the shore. It was odd, considering he'd grown up in the desert, how the sight and sound of the ocean could calm him. Yet from the first time Dean had stepped into the sea with his bare feet, he had fallen in love, vowing to find a place by the ocean he could call home.

Staying in his apartment had been out of the question. Dean had woken up by himself and in a full-blown panic. Sloane's presence had soothed any fears or worries he might have had, but without him, Dean's mind had been left to wander over all the horrible possibilities and uncertainties he'd built up in his head.

That was until he'd laid eyes on the propped-up paper on the bedside table, with the familiar handwriting on the front.

It's okay. Read this.

While Dean had still felt the scramble of panic at Sloane's absence, he had taken the message to heart. Forcing himself to calm down, Dean had pushed himself out of bed, leaving the letter where it sat. Despite its attempts at comfort, Dean had put it off while he brewed a cup of coffee, washed his face, and pulled on a pair of loose pants and a shirt.

Only when he had the first sips of coffee in his system did Dean finally sit down and allow himself to grab the letter. It had taken longer than he was willing to admit to unfold the paper and read it. The letter was still in his pocket as he watched the waves. He'd read it enough times, short as it was, to the point of having memorized each word.

D*EAN*,

Sorry, I didn't wake you. You were sleeping so good, I couldn't. Sorry to leave you, but I had to get to my shift. Otherwise, I would have stayed.

I promise I'm not running or hiding. Last night was wonderful, and it's given me so much to think about. I'll be back after my shift is over, I swear. We'll sit down and talk about this. There's so much I want to say.

I'll be back,
Sloane.

I*T WAS MORE* than Dean could have hoped for, but not quite enough. Sloane had promised he'd be back, which was enough to quell the worst of Dean's terrors. Yet, he hadn't said anything more than that.

Did it mean Sloane had enjoyed himself but wanted nothing more? Had it been enough for Sloane not to hate Dean, but he was still backing away? He might still lose his friend, which was the greatest terror Dean possessed.

Dean shook his head, knowing he was making no sense but unable to stop himself. At the root of everything was the terror that he would lose Sloane. Even if the night had been the realization of his greatest fantasies and hopes, Dean would gladly give it all away so long as he had Sloane in his life. To lose Sloane as a lover, as a boyfriend, as a potential husband, Dean could live with. Even though he had come so much closer than ever, he could deal with losing the chance at something more.

But to lose Sloane completely.

Dean closed his arms around his middle, shaking his head slowly. If Sloane were going to leave forever, he would have done so without leaving a note. It was too easy to listen to the voice inside him that told him Sloane was just being nice, but that wasn't fair. Sloane deserved better than that, and Dean knew, in his heart of hearts, Sloane would never do anything just to spare his feelings.

Initially, Sloane had put him off with how blunt and short he was, yet Dean had come to appreciate that part of his friend. Sloane might not have tact, but Dean had always known where Sloane stood. Sure, the man might hide behind a wall of grumpiness and coarse language, but at the end of the day, Dean knew how Sloane truly felt, and he never had to feel that Sloane was lying to him to spare his feelings.

And he wasn't going to start now.

Easier said than done, but Dean shook his head as the darker thoughts crowded into his brain. Rather than give them attention, Dean dug into his pocket and pulled out his phone. He wasn't sure when Sloane was getting off his shift, as it could change daily, but six seemed like a safe time. Dean wanted to be back in time to find Sloane there as per his promise, and since it was fifteen minutes away from that time, he slid off the rock he was sitting on.

"Here we go," Dean muttered as he made his way back.

* * *

I'M STRAIGHT, RIGHT?

Stepping through his door, Dean stopped. A pair of huge but familiar boots sat beside the door. Sloane always made his boots sit so meticulously, even placing the laces on the insides to ensure they weren't tripped over. The realization that the man was in the house sent Dean's heart fluttering.

Swallowing hard, Dean closed the door, dropping his keys in the bowl. Not bothering to take his shoes off, he stepped further into his apartment, listening for sounds of life. He stopped at the doorway to the living room, spotting a huge shape on the couch. The blinds of the glass sliding door had been drawn, but Dean could see Sloane's outline.

His eyes adjusted to the dim light, and he realized Sloane was out cold. For a moment, Dean wondered how long Sloane had been there before remembering how easily Sloane could drop off. It was a skill Dean had learned to master during his deployment, taking sleep where he could, but he wasn't quite as good at it off the field. Sloane had always joked that he'd learned it long before joining the military, and Basic had honed the skill to a whole new level.

Dean stepped closer, careful not to make any sudden noise and startle Sloane awake. Smiling, he reached down, adjusting the collar of Sloane's shirt so it wasn't bound around his neck quite as tightly. Dean had always teased Sloane that he looked so much less grumpy when sleeping, but honestly, Dean never thought Sloane looked all that mean. To him, Sloane was Sloane, and his handsome features, awake or asleep, eased an ache in Dean's chest every time.

Content to let Sloane rest, Dean carefully ran his fingers over Sloane's arm before retreating to his room. His nerves tightened when Sloane's hand closed around his wrist, startling him with the sudden movement. In an instant, his tension evaporated as Sloane's sleepy face peered up at him, smiling.

"Hey," Sloane croaked, his fingers stroking Dean's skin.

"Didn't mean to wake you," Dean whispered.

Sloane shook his head. "I was only catching a bit of sleep while waiting for you."

"You could have texted me," Dean said.

Sloane chuckled, releasing Dean's hand so he could stretch. "I didn't mind waiting."

Dean's eyes flicked to where Sloane's shirt rode up, showing his flat stomach and the tantalizing trail of hair that disappeared beneath his waistline. It wasn't the first time he'd found himself doing it, and there was still that instinctive curl of discomfort at checking his friend out. What was new was the realization that he'd had his hands all over that part of Sloane's body and elsewhere. Despite years of telling himself to be careful, not to be obvious, and to keep it quiet, Dean let his eyes linger on Sloane a moment longer before looking at his face again.

Sloane raised a brow, smirking. "Yeah?"

Dean ducked his head. "Sorry."

Sloane chuckled, reaching to take hold of Dean's wrist again. "Don't be. I kind of like it."

Dean looked up. "Yeah?"

Sloane pulled him close until Dean had no choice but to plop down on the small space left on the edge of the couch. Sloane's body pressed against his back, warm and relaxed from his nap. So close, Dean could smell Sloane's woodsy cologne, hinting of rich wood and fertile land, with just a dash of something spicy and enticing. He'd always loved that smell, but having smelled it while Sloane thrust deep inside him made the scent so much more appealing.

Sloane smiled, shifting his grip to hold Dean's hand. "That surprise you?"

"It doesn't you?" Dean asked incredulously.

"I've never believed in lying to you, Dean, so I won't tell you it isn't a little weird for me."

Dean nodded, not surprised but hating the sinking feeling in his gut. Despite everything that had happened between him and Sloane, he shouldn't have expected anything less. Sloane was straight, of course. The idea of being checked out by a guy, having slept with a guy, and everything else would be weird.

Sloane watched his face, still smiling gently. "But that doesn't mean I don't like it."

"That doesn't make a lot of sense, does it?" Dean asked.

Sloane snorted. "Did it make sense for you to have been into me all this time?"

Dean frowned. "I never said it made sense."

Sloane shook his head. "Look, I didn't mean anything against you. I just meant sometimes, we feel things that don't make sense, but they are what they are, right? It didn't make sense for you to feel the way you did about me all that time, but you did. Maybe you felt that way for a reason because you sensed something I didn't even think could exist, or maybe hearts simply do what they want, and we've got to deal with the mess they make."

Dean nodded slowly, understanding Sloane even as he smiled at the realization that his friend was babbling. Sloane had never been good at expressing himself verbally, which was probably why the physical affection element of their friendship had always been the strongest. Sloane didn't consider himself a good speaker, but he could get his point across by hugging Dean or letting Dean lay his head in Sloane's lap.

"My point is, yeah, this is a little weird for me. Of course, it is. You know I tried watching gay porn after...the whole blowjob thing?" Sloane asked, averting his eyes.

Dean couldn't help his snort. "Seriously?"

"Yeah, I tried a few videos, including a couple I don't want to discuss. Didn't do anything for me."

"Well, you're not gay," Dean said, proud of himself for keeping his voice free of sadness or worry.

Sloane nodded. "I mean, those videos did nothing, not even a twitch from my dick. The minute I started thinking about you giving me a blowjob, though, I was hard in two seconds flat."

Dean blinked. "You got hard from that?"

"Got more than hard."

It took a minute before Dean understood what he meant. "You...jerked off to that memory?"

Sloane shrugged. "It was a good blowjob."

Dean looked down at their joined hands, sorting through his thoughts. On the one hand, it was incredibly hot to think that Sloane had pleasured himself to the memory of Dean's impulsive, drunken blowjob. On the other hand, it was also bizarre to think that Sloane, a man Dean knew to be nothing but straight, had been aroused and got off to the thought of a guy, Dean specifically, blowing him.

Dean gave a low chuckle. "Alright, I'm starting to get the weirdness here now, too."

"Right? I can watch different dudes go at it and feel nothing. I mean, I can see a dude who's good-looking and know he's good-looking, but it doesn't do anything for me. But I remembered that night, and I was ready to go. And last night? Jesus, Dean, that was...it was—"

Dean looked up, unable to stop himself from worrying his bottom lip as he waited for Sloane to find what he wanted to say. Whatever came out of Sloane's mouth next would determine where they were headed. Despite everything they'd done so far, Dean couldn't shake the dread that it was all for nothing. That, in the end, despite how much 'fun' Sloane had, he would back away from it all, and they'd continue their lives as they had before.

Sloane reached behind him, flicking on the lamp beside the couch. Dean winced against the sudden glare, waiting till he could see better before opening his eyes fully. Sloane looked him over with the strangest expression, both hungry and awed.

"What?" Dean asked self-consciously.

"None of those guys did it, but just sitting here, looking at you, touching you gets my brain going all over again. I've always liked being close to you and touching you, and maybe that was a sign. I didn't realize what that touch could be until last night. Because last night was just...fucking amazing, Dean."

Dean felt heat rise in his cheeks. "I'm not arguing, but—"

"I don't know what that makes me or if it makes me anything. Maybe I'm straight for everyone else but you?"

Dean let out a nervous chuckle. "Sounds, uh, too good to be true."

Sloane cocked his head, gaze going soft. "You don't believe me."

"I do," Dean was quick to assure him.

"I wouldn't say this to make you feel better."

Dean shook his head, knowing that was true. "No, you wouldn't."

"And I'm not going to say shit like this unless I'm sure. One hundred percent sure."

Dean's shoulders slumped. "I know."

"It might be weird because I never saw it coming, but you know what's weirdest about it?"

"That I have a dick?" Dean offered with a light, jittery laugh.

"You'd think that, but no, dude, you not having boobs, having a lot more body hair than I'm used to, and being all muscle doesn't bother me. It's *you*, why would it bother me? And that's the weird thing. This doesn't feel much different from what we were doing before. You've always been you, and I like you for you. Now, I just happen to like you in a different way. I don't think anyone but you could have made me feel like this about them."

Dean's stuttering heart slowed, and his muscles relaxed as the full effect of Sloane's words washed over him. The backs of his eyes pricked, and he sucked in a sharp breath as he took in the softness of Sloane's gaze.

"Really?" Dean croaked.

"And I'm pretty sure I was jealous of Marco."

That jerked a snort from Dean. "Seriously?"

Sloane wrapped his arm around Dean's waist and pulled him closer. "Yeah, really. Didn't feel like it at the time, but I don't think I liked him being with you. But this, this holding you thing? It feels right like it always has. And last night? That was the extra step with what we've been doing. It all feels right, and my brain thinks that's weird, but my heart knows it's right."

Dean had always known Sloane had a sentimental streak that stretched far wider than the man was willing to admit. Usually, Dean would make a joke, and Sloane would tease him back, and they would continue their lives. But, held in Sloane's arms, knowing the words were genuine and aimed directly at him, Dean found himself at a loss for words.

Sloane searched his face. "I know it will take a little time for us to get over the weirdness, and there's still things to work through. But while I might not have everything figured out, I know that if you'll have me, I want to be with you. I want you. Everything you're willing to give, I want, and everything I've got, it's yours."

"Holy shit," Dean whispered, feeling lightheaded.

"Is that a yes?" Sloane asked.

I'M STRAIGHT, RIGHT?

"Fuck, yes. That's a yes," Dean said in a rush.

Sloane's face broke into a wide grin, and he pulled Dean toward him. Dean's heart caught in his throat as, without even the slightest hesitation, Sloane pulled him into a deep kiss. Heat radiated out from Dean's chest, washing through him and flaring into bright points of sheer pleasure where his body pressed against Sloane's. He clutched onto Sloane, desperate to feel the reassurance, the reality that his dreams had finally come true.

"Mine," Sloane whispered, stroking his hand through Dean's hair.

"Yours."

EPILOGUE

1 Year Later

Sloane bent over his desk, squinting at the note. For the life of him, he couldn't make out the chicken scratch, no matter how much he squinted. He picked the post-it note up, holding it closer to the light to see if that would help, but it was useless.

"Hey, Sloane, your shift is over, man. What the hell are you doing still here?" Simmons asked from the doorway to Sloane's office.

Sloane rolled his eyes. "Easy for you to say. You weren't left with paperwork a mile high. Is this your chicken scratch?"

Simmons leaned forward. "Oh, yeah. It was telling you General Winter wanted to speak to you but didn't say what for. I left it because you'd wandered off again."

Wandering seemed to be the bulk of his job. Sloane had been more than happy to shift into the military police if he didn't have to sit in the guardhouse anymore. What he hadn't known was that he was going to eventually get put in the control seat of the damn thing. He'd gone from being bored in a guardhouse to making sure his soldiers behaved and tossing the drunk ones in the drunk tank for the night.

Sloane looked up in disbelief. "You're the guy's assistant or whatever you want to call it. How do you not know what he wanted?"

Simmons scowled. "I'm his liaison first of all, and secondly, I don't know all his business."

Sloane didn't believe it for a minute, though he let it drop. He wasn't sure exactly *how* Simmons had gone from a grunt on constant guard duty to the liaison for the general, but he couldn't argue with the results of the change. Simmons was considerably more agreeable than he'd ever been, and despite being quieter than before, he also seemed happier. Sloane had attempted to broach the subject of Simmons' dating life, but all he'd got in return so far was a sly smile.

"Is he in right now?" Sloane asked.

Simmons snorted. "No, you'll have to call him back tomorrow. Which again, means you should probably head out before something else comes up. Plus, your man is waiting for you outside."

Sloane stood up. "You could have fucking led with that."

Simmons laughed, backing out of the room and out of Sloane's reach. "Yeah, but watching big, mean, grumpy Sloane turn into a sap instantly is fun."

"Get the fuck out of my office," Sloane growled, slamming the note down on his desk.

Simmons laughed his way out of the office, with Sloane close behind. There was nothing left for him to deal with anyway, not anything that couldn't be handled the next day.

Irritated, he shoved the door leading outside open, and sure enough, Dean was waiting. The sight of his boyfriend hunched over on a bench, tapping away on his phone, soothed Sloane's annoyance. The tip of Dean's tongue was sticking out between his lips as he typed, a sure sign he was focused on whatever he was trying to write.

"Howdy, handsome," Sloane said as he approached.

Dean looked up, face breaking into a smile. "Hey, you're early."

Sloane snorted. "Early? I was supposed to get out of here half an hour ago."

"Yeah, early for you."

"I don't like it when you're right."

Dean chuckled, pocketing his phone before standing up. "I think you do."

Sloane reached down, taking hold of Dean's hip and pulling him close. The last of his irritation disappeared instantly as Dean's body folded against his perfectly. Sloane was never sure if their bodies fit so well naturally or if he and Dean were so in sync that it just happened. Personally, Sloane didn't care what it was. It was one of the best feelings in the world.

Dean leaned up, catching Sloane's lips with his and kissing him gently. The press of Dean's lips was soft at first, but Sloane felt Dean's body coil up as though preparing to strike. A moment later, the kiss deepened, and Sloane could practically feel the barely restrained need pouring from Dean's body as he pushed just a little bit closer.

And there was another one of Sloane's favorite feelings in the world.

"You sleep?" Sloane asked as he pulled away.

Dean smiled, dropping down to flat feet once more. "I got a couple of hours before I came over."

Sloane slid his hand down, resting it on Dean's lower back. "Maybe after I shower, you can have another hour or two while we watch a cheesy movie?"

"Better plan. I help you with that shower, and then we watch an awesome movie."

"Somehow, I don't think you'll be helping me with my shower."

"No, but I'll help you with something."

Before everything had changed for them, Sloane had never thought of Dean as a particularly sexual person. Sure, Dean had mentioned getting laid occasionally, and Sloane knew he had to have desires. But it wasn't until he and Sloane started dating, and Dean grew comfortable, more assured that they would be a couple for a while, that Sloane got to see what Dean had been keeping from him.

To his absolute delight, Sloane had discovered Dean was incredibly sexual. Then again, Sloane would have found it impossible not to be turned on by someone who was aroused at just the sight of him as Dean seemed to be. Sloane thought that maybe once the sparkle of being with Sloane had worn off, Dean might ease back considerably. There had, of course, been a bit of slackening as the months went by, but never enough to make Sloane wonder or worry.

Sloane led Dean away from the bench and back toward their apartment. "Who were you texting?"

Dean snickered. "Your mom."

"Why is that funny?"

"She's asking me when I'm going to make an honest man out of you."

"An honest...she's trying to get you to propose?"

"I think she's trying to get me to talk to you about marriage so that one of us proposes."

Sloane sighed. "I'll talk to her, good God."

"Don't. She's happy as hell that we're together, and she's only saying it to be supportive in her own way. Let her have her fun."

Sloane eyed him, curious. "*Do* you want to get married?"

"To you?"

Sloane scowled. "Yes, to me."

"You know, in all the times I wondered what it would be like to be with you, I never actually thought about marriage."

"Really?"

"That surprises you?"

Sloane shrugged. "You're the romantic one, and hell, I've thought about it before, so I figured you had."

Dean stopped, turning to face Sloane with a smirk. "Wait, me? I'm the romantic one, not you?"

"Yeah, so?" Sloane asked in bewilderment.

"You, the man who makes sure my coffee is brewed and set to go by the time I wake up?"

"You're a zombie when you wake up."

"Or when you ordered me some chocolate from Switzerland because I said it sounded delicious?"

"You like chocolate and were being stubborn about ordering some."

"Remember when I sprained my wrist, and you came over and did my laundry and dishes when I was at the clinic?"

"It's not like you could do it."

Dean shook his head. "You're a sap."

"It's practical?"

Dean leaned in, kissing the bottom of Sloane's chin. "Sap."

Sloane huffed before kissing the tip of Dean's nose. "For you."

If he hadn't been a sap before, the pure joy in Dean's sudden smile would have certainly made him one. God, the man was so beautiful it hurt Sloane in the best way possible. How he had somehow missed what was right there between them, he would never know.

Dean reached out, taking Sloane's hand. "So, marriage, huh?"

Sloane grinned, following happily after Dean, casting his

bittersweet thoughts aside. Their time together hadn't been a waste in Sloane's mind, only the precursor to something even greater. Now they were together, they had all the time in the world to discover what wonderful things awaited them.

And Sloane was going to love every second of it.

ABOUT THE AUTHOR

Romeo Alexander lives in Michigan, USA, with his dog and two cats. As a certified night owl, coffee and a wicked sense of humor keep him going most days, as does playing with flavors in the kitchen.

As a gay man, he believes in writing about what you know whenever possible; his stories come from the heart and with a dose of humor thrown in. His characters grapple with relationships, emotions, and real-world issues, good and bad, using their hearts as a guiding compass to get their all-important happy ever after.

Printed in Great Britain
by Amazon